# CAMPTOWN RACES

## And other stories from
## Camptown, Kentucky

# CAMPTOWN RACES

## And other stories from Camptown, Kentucky

## Kenn Grimes

Deer Lake Press
Boyne City, Michigan

Publisher
Deer Lake Press
715 E. Deer Lake Rd.
Boyne City, Michigan, 49712
deerlakepress@aol.com

Editions ISBN 978-0-9860020-4-5
Soft cover
Contact the author at kenngrimesauthor@aol.com

# DEDICATION

To the memory of my oldest and closest friend,

**Al Evans**

with whom I spent countless summer days
racing up and down the alley behind our
two houses playing basketball.
I miss you, Al.

# CONTENTS

# Other books
# by

## KENN GRIMES

Camptown . . . one hundred and fifty years of stories
From Camptown, Kentucky

The Other Side of Yesterday

Ancestors

The Whipping Post

To save us all from Satan's power

## THE BOOKER FALLS MYSTERY SERIES

Strangled in the Stacks

Trifecta of Murder

Paint the Librarian Dead

Cold-Hearted Corpse

## THE IOU
### 1847, 1997

Nick carefully lifted the battered lid of the cigar box. He'd seen the box just once before, in 1955, when he was twelve and his father brought it home from the bank vault, its resting place for almost sixty years, ever since Nick's grandfather's death in 1898. Now, forty-two years later, Nick's own father had died.

He studied the inside of the lid: a picture of a black man with a pair of glasses propped on his head—the same picture as the top of the lid. The brand was Old Virginia Cheroots, made by P. Lorillard. He recognized the name Lorillard, but not the brand. Did they still make them? How old was the box? He didn't know.

He reached in and withdrew a scrap of paper followed by two letters, each rolled up and tied with a ribbon. The last item was a small leather pouch from which Nick removed two coins, one carefully wrapped in cellophane, the other loose. For a few moments, he studied both coins, turning them over in his fingers. The loose one was a well-worn, large U.S. Cent, dated 1847; the second a fifty-cent piece dated 1865, with an "S" mintmark.

The letters were old, yellowed by the years, and yet still in excellent shape. After all, they had been handled no more than a half dozen times since they'd been written.

He picked up the scrap of paper and read it.

"IOU one cent. A. Lincoln."

One of the letters was next. Nick knew it was written by his great-grandfather, a second lieutenant in the 6th Kentucky Cavalry, to his wife, Nick's great-grandmother, the day before he was killed at the Battle of Chickamauga. He began to read:

*September 17, 1863*

*My dearest Rebecca,*

*I received your letter of July 15th and it relieved my heart to find all is well with you and Micah. You must know how I miss both of you and wish I was with you right now. One day this terrible war will end and life will be normal again.*

*A strange occurrence happened today. I met a Lieutenant Johnson from another company who was wearing one of those buttons from Mr. Lincoln's campaign a few years back with his picture on it. When I saw it I realized it was the same A. Lincoln who had give me the IOU when I was nine years old.*

*I remember mentioning that to you once but now I feel compelled to put down in writing what transpired that day so if something should happen to me—but it won't, I know that—our son should know that one day his father shook the hand of President Abraham Lincoln. Before he was president, of course.*

*Please put this missive in a place of safe keeping. Upon my return I will read it to our son.*

*Your loving husband, William*

Nick laid the letter aside and picked up the account that had accompanied it. As he read his great-grandfather's account of his encounter with A. Lincoln, Nick felt himself slipping back in time, back through the years . . . back to 1847.

From my vantage point in front of the Tipsy Toad Saloon I watched as he came slowly down the street, a tall, gangly man riding a horse that seemed much too small for him.

When he came to my father's livery stable he stopped, dismounted, and tied the horse to the hitching post.

"What can I do for you, friend?" asked my father, stepping out from the building.

"Might I tie my horse here?" asked the stranger. "I desire to quench my thirst at the saloon, but their post seems to be filled."

My father looked across the street to where I stood, frowning when he saw me there. "I don't take much for drinking," he said.

"Nor do I," said the stranger. "All I desire is a mug of sarsaparilla."

My father's face broadened into a grin. "By all means, feel free to leave the horse here. Do you need him cared for?"

"Thank you, no. I've come just from Lexington. He's still quite fresh."

Father nodded and walked back into the stable.

As the man approached me I glanced at his boots. My sole purpose for being in front of the saloon was to make a little money by shining the boots and shoes of the men as they came and went.

I could see that the stranger's boots were, indeed, candidates for my labor.

"How about a shine, mister?" I asked as he stepped up onto the wooden sidewalk. "Just one cent."

"One cent, you say," said the man.

Although he wasn't the handsomest man I'd ever seen—indeed, perhaps the homeliest—there was something about his face that put me at ease.

"Why not?" he said. He placed one foot up on my box.

"You just passing through town?" I asked.

"I'm visiting my wife's family in Lexington," he said.

"You don't live there?"

"No, I used to live in Illinois, but I've recently moved to Washington."

"The capital?" I asked, looking up. "I always wanted to go there."

"That's right," he said. "I've just been elected to congress."

I wasn't sure what congress was, but I supposed it to be something of importance.

"Appears to be quite a spate of new building going on here in town," said the man.

Without stopping my work I looked around. It was true. For years, even before I was born, Camptown served two purposes: a place for the stagecoach to stop for passengers to quench their thirst and get a bite to eat at the Tipsy Toad while my pa tended to their horses; and the site of the horse races held there each year. Hundreds of people from all over Kentucky—maybe farther away, as far as I knew—came and pitched tents out in the woods, setting up little camps that lasted two or three weeks. I reckon that's how it came to be called Camptown, 'cause there sure hadn't been no actual town, only the saloon and my pa's livery stable.

Then last January Mr. Little, who owns a big spread over by Crownsville, a few miles away from Camptown, decided to build a sawmill on the Chickapea River. Overnight other buildings sprouted up like mushrooms in the spring.

Now the main street where we were boasted more than a dozen businesses.

"Yep," I said. "Reckon one of these days we'll be as big as Lexington."

The man smiled.

"Son, that's about the finest shine a pair of boots ever received," he said when I finished. He reached his hand inside his coat pocket. A look of concern crossed his face. He thrust his hand into the other pockets of his coat and pants.

"I fear I find myself in an awkward position," he said at last. "It appears I have left my purse back at the house. If you will trust me to

4

*leave and get it, I will return posthaste to pay you the agreed-upon amount."*

*I looked at him. I knew it was a good two-hour ride to Lexington, and another two back. And I had no doubt he would make the ride to pay me what he owed me. But I also figured I could trust him.*

*"Heck, that's all right, mister," I said. "Why don't you just pay me the next time you're in town. You got an honest face—I trust you."*

*The man smiled again, an even bigger smile than before.*

*"What is your name, my good sir?" he asked.*

*"Will," I answered. "Will Van Pelt."*

*"And how old are you, Will?"*

*"Nine, sir."*

*"I have two sons. Robert is four and young Eddie was born this past year. I hope when they're your age they will be as trusting and charitable as you are. Master Will, where might I find some writing paper and a pen?"*

*"My pa owns the livery stable. He's always got paper and pencils laying around. I reckon a pen, too."*

*"I'll be right back," said the man. He turned and strode across the street to the stable.*

*Minutes later he returned, paper and pen in hand. Using the top of a barrel, he wrote something, then handed the paper to me. I looked at it: "IOU one cent. A. Lincoln."*

*"Heck, this ain't necessary," I said.*

*"Perhaps not," said the man. "But now you have it in writing that I am in debt to you, and not only for the penny. You saved me from the great embarrassment of having purchased and consumed my drink at the tavern, here, and then being unable to pay for it."*

*"Okay," I said.*

*The man reached out his hand for me to shake. It was a big hand, and bony, but strong. I took it and we shook.*

*"I look forward to seeing you again, Master Will."*

*"Likewise," I said.*

He walked back across the street, untied his horse, mounted, and rode out of town, the same way he'd come in.

And that was my meeting with A. Lincoln. Little did I know one day he would be president, and I would be a soldier in his army.

∞

Nick picked up the last letter, untied the ribbon, and began to read.

*April 14, 1865*
*Dear Master Will,*

*I trust this letter finds you in good health. And, if you are reading it, then my courier was successful in locating you.*

*You perhaps do not remember our meeting eighteen years ago, there in Camptown. You provided me with a shoeshine, and when I discovered, to my embarrassment, I left my purse behind in Lexington, you were kind enough to extend me credit for the one cent I owed you, even though I was a complete stranger.*

*In truth, I must admit I, myself, had forgotten all about that debt until last night, when I had a most unsettling dream, one in which I found myself standing before Saint Peter at the Pearly Gates, waiting to be admitted. When he advised me I could not enter until all my debts had been discharged, I started to inform him that I was in debt to no man. Then I remembered our encounter. And that was when I awoke.*

*Enclosed in the pouch that my courier has delivered you will find the money I owe you. As a means of providing interest for this debt that has taken so many years to repay, I have also enclosed a fifty cent piece from our mint in San Francisco, a city I very much look forward to visiting one day. This coin was presented to me recently by Mr. Pollock, our Director of the Mint, who informed me it is a sample coin, a proof I believe he called it. I had thought to give the coin to Tad as a keepsake, but knowing his propensity for purchasing candy, fear it would not be long in his possession.*

*You may choose to spend the penny, although I am aware a penny does not buy much these days. The other coin you may wish to keep, however, as someday it may have some value.*

*I know not when that day will come when I shall meet my maker but I know now I can do so truly free of debt or obligation to any man, and once again I thank you profusely for the trust you showed in me.*

*I must close this letter now, as I have a meeting with my cabinet and with General Grant in a few minutes. Though the day promises to be a busy one, I am looking forward to this evening, and attending the theatre with Mrs. Lincoln.*

*Gratefully yours, A. Lincoln*

Nick let his eyes wander over the items spread out before him, mementos passed down from generation to generation. Certainly, they had monetary value, particularly the IOU and the letter, both signed by Lincoln, not to mention a coin so rare that, according to coin catalogs, it never existed.

But their value went far beyond money. They were a part of history, of the history of his family. And now they were his responsibility.

With great care, he re-rolled the letters, tying each with its timeworn ribbon. He replaced the coins in the leather pouch and returned everything to its resting place in the cigar box.

He stood and walked over to the double glass doors that led out onto the balcony of his apartment which encompassed the entire third floor of the building that had replaced his great-great-grandfather's livery in 1913 and looked across the street to the sidewalk in front of the Tipsy Toad Bar and Grill, to the exact spot where his great-grandfather shined Abraham Lincoln's boots a century and a half earlier.

One hundred and fifty years, thought Nick. So many changes. So many memories. So many stories.

## CAMPTOWN RACES
### 1849

George sat in his rocker on the front porch, enjoying the late afternoon sun on his face. It was an unusually mild day for this time of year. Max, a Blue Tick Hound and the old man's constant companion, lay asleep at his feet.

George had almost nodded off, too, when the blast from the horn of an automobile coming up the road toward the house roused him.

Max didn't stir.

A beat-up Oldsmobile, trailing a cloud of dust, came to a sudden stop five yards from the porch steps, and two children, a boy and a girl, tumbled out from the rear seat.

George smiled. It was always a treat to see his granddaughter and her two children. At ninety-two—or maybe ninety-three, he didn't know for sure—and with failing eyesight, he no longer was able to drive. He depended on Dolores to bring the children, Howard, eleven, and Ethel, eight, out to visit him, which she did as often as possible. But her position as principal of the only Negro school in Shawneetown, some two hours away, afforded little extra time for making the trip out to her grandfather's farm.

"Papaw!" the children shouted, almost in unison.

"Hey, younguns!" said George, "get on up here, and give

8

your Papaw some sugar."

But the children didn't need an invitation. Before the words hardly left the old man's mouth, both of them bounded up the steps and wrapped their arms around him. Max opened one eye and looked up to see what the ruckus was all about.

"Hey, Papaw, how are you?" asked Dolores, emerging from the car.

"I'm fine, honey, just fine. Come on up. There's some coffee on the stove if you want some. Maybe the children would like some Dr. Pepper. I know I do."

"We come out—" Howard began.

"We *came* out," corrected his mother, on her way into the house to get the drinks.

"We *came* out to ride Gingerbread Lady," said Howard, plopping down next to Ethel on the porch swing that hung suspended from the ceiling,

"And to see me, I hope?" asked George, a grin on his face.

"*And* to see you, Papaw," said Ethel, "and to hear the story again."

"*What* story?" But he knew what story they wanted to hear.

"The one about how you got freed and got Lucy," said Howard.

"Whatchoo wanta hear dat ol' story again, fo'?" asked George, a twinkle in his eye. "I done told y'all dat story 'bout a hunnert times already."

"We *love* that story," said Ethel. "Please, Papaw, tell it to us again."

"Well, okay, if you *really* want to hear it."

"We do, we do!" squealed the children.

George leaned back in his rocker and closed his eyes..

"It was back in '49," he said. "I was a few years older dan Howard, here, maybe tirteen or fo'teen." It seemed like only yesterday.

"What's your horse's name, boy?"

"Oh, ain't mah hawse, suh. B'longs to mah mastah, Marse Roberts."

"What's the name of Marse Roberts's horse, then?"

"Lucy, suh. Her name is Lucy."

"Do you know how old Lucy is?"

"Don' rightly know, suh. I reckon as how she done been wit Marse Roberts since 'fore I come to live on his farm."

"And how old are you, boy?"

"Tirteen, fo'teen . . . I ain't rightly certain, suh."

"Is the horse going to race?"

George had come to Camptown with his and Lucy's owner, Jig Roberts, for the horse races, an annual event that spanned six days, Monday through Saturday. The course was laid out to run from Camptown to Crownsville, a distance of about two and a half miles. From Crownsville another course of equal length led back to Camptown, creating a complete lap five miles in length, enough to test the mettle of any horse. In addition, many races were ten miles, as the horses made two complete laps of five miles each. Over the years, more than one steed took its final breath somewhere between the two towns. At most meets, so many horses competed that torches atop ten-foot poles were placed at intervals along the course, which allowed racing into the night, sometimes into the wee hours of the morning.

Hundreds of people from all over Kentucky and neighboring states came to watch the Camptown Races, to wager on which horses would win and, sometimes, which would even finish.

Fine ladies in hoop skirts and Garibaldi dresses sat in their carriages and wagon beds near the finish line, brandishing

10

parasols to shield their delicate skin from the hot August sun. Elaborately decorated hand-held fans served both in keeping the air moving around them and also, for the younger, unattached women, an important role in flirting.

Many of the men were attired as grandly as the ladies, although there were always a goodly number of farmers in overalls and straw hats present, convinced their horse—the same one that had pulled their wagon into town—could outrun the gentlemen's thoroughbreds. Nearby, slaves kept busy preparing lunches and cold drinks for the spectators.

This was George's first time at the races. In years past Jig always brought Willoughby, a slave who had been in the Roberts's household for over thirty years. The previous winter, however, Willoughby had contracted typhoid fever and died. Since George had been entrusted with Lucy's care following Willoughby's death, he had been tapped to take his place here at the races.

But Lucy was definitely not a racehorse. At twelve years of age, she appeared to be well past the point of doing any racing at all. Her sole purpose was as transportation for George. It was Roberts's horse, Cinnamon, that was the true racehorse.

"Oh, no, suh. She ain't runnin'. She too ol' to run. She jus' a ol' bob-tailed nag, dat's all she is."

The man pushed Lucy's lip up with his hand to inspect her teeth. He slowly walked all around her, ran his hands over her body, and lifted her legs to inspect them.

"I think she could run," he said when he finished his inspection.

George started to laugh but quickly stopped himself. He didn't want to offend the man and risk a beating.

"In fact," the man continued, turning to his companion, a younger man who had remained silent during the entire exchange, "I'd be willing to bet on her."

11

George's jaw dropped. "You would?"

"Go get your master and bring him over here," said the man. "Let's see what we can work out."

*****

"You want me to do *what?*"

Jig Roberts wasn't sure he'd heard the man correctly.

"I want you to race your mare," said the man, "against Colonel Maguire's bay."

"You must be out of your mind," said Jig. "I've seen that bay run. He ain't the fastest horse in the world, but he's a helluva lot faster than my mare."

"I've seen the bay run, too," said the man. "I think your mare can take him. And I'm willing to put money on it."

"Well, *I* ain't," said Jig. "I'd have to put up fifty dollars for the purse. No way I'm about to do that."

"How about if I put up the purse, and give you half when we win?"

"*When* we win? You're pretty damn confident, ain't you?"

"I have a feeling about this horse," said the man.

"Yeah, well I do, too. And my feeling is the poor thing'd drop dead before she got back to Camptown. That is, if she even made it to Crownsville. I ain't about to make myself look like a fool, racing this old nag."

"All right, then, how about selling her to me?"

"Sell her? You wanta *buy* her?"

"That's right. I'll buy her from you, and I'll race her."

"*You* gonna ride her?"

"No, I'll get one of the boys to ride her. How about your boy, here?" he asked, nodding toward George.

"Tell you what," said Jig. "I'm a little hard up for cash right now, and I'm purty sure my filly can win a couple races. Thing

12

is, I need money for the purses. I'll sell you the nigger, and throw the horse in for free."

The man looked at George, then at Jig.

"I don't believe in slavery. Never did own one."

"Then this here be your chance," said Jig. "Otherwise, I'm a keepin' the horse."

The man thought for a minute, then asked, "How much?"

"I can let you have him for a thousand."

The man let out a whistle.

"That's pretty steep."

"Just look at the boy. He's young, he's healthy, he's strong. Hell, you could probably take him down to Naw'luns and get twice that. Or, set him free if you want. I don't care."

The man looked at George again.

"Can you ride this animal?" he asked.

"Whatchoo mean, 'ride him'? You mean, like in a race?" asked George.

"Yes. In a race."

George wrinkled his eyebrows.

"Don' know," he said. "I s'pose. But I don' tink dis ol' nag could do nuttin' in a race."

"Let me be the judge of that," said the man. "I'll give you seven hundred," he said, turning back to Jig.

"Aw, hell no," exclaimed Jig. "He's worth a lot more'n that."

"Seven, fifty;" said the man, "not a penny more."

Jig frowned. He started to protest but decided seven hundred and fifty dollars was probably the best he was going to get.

"Sold," he said. "I'll draw up the papers on both the nigger and the horse."

While Jig walked back to his wagon to get paper and pen, the man turned to George once more.

13

"My name is Mr. Marbury. My friend here is Mr. Foster. What's your name, son?"

"George, suh."

"All right, George, you get a good night's sleep, because first thing tomorrow morning we're going to race Lucy here against Maguire's bay."

*****

But George was too excited to sleep. He decided to join the other slaves who had gathered around a big bonfire they'd built in a clearing in the woods. He was surprised to see the gentleman introduced to him as Mr. Foster standing by himself at the clearing's edge. But he gave the man's presence little thought. It was the music that caught his attention.

"What be dat song dey all singin'?" he asked a young girl perched next to him on the log.

"Ain't got no name, fer as I know," said the girl.

George listened to the music, fascinated.

*De Camptown darkies sing dis song*
*Doo-dah! Doo-dah!*
*De Camptown racetrack five mile long*
*Oh! Doo-dah day!*
*Come down heah wid my hat caved in*
*Doo-dah! Doo-dah!*
*Back home I go wid a pocket full a tin*
*Oh! Doo-dah day!*
*De long tail mare and de big black hoss*
*Doo-dah! Doo-dah!*
*Dey fly de track and dey bōt cut across*
*Oh! Doo-dah day!*

*De blind hoss sticken in a big mud hole*
*Doo-dah! Doo-dah!*
*Cain't touch bottom wid a ten-foot pole*
*Oh! Doo-dah day!*

"What dat mean, dat 'doo-dah'?" asked George.

"Don' mean nothin'," the girl answered. "Jus' nonsense words."

George sat for hours, listening to the singing. At last, exhaustion overtook him. He stood and walked back to where Lucy was bedded down for the night next to the two men's carriage, laid down beside her and fell fast asleep.

*****

"George, get up."

George opened his eyes to see Mr. Marbury and Mr. Foster standing over him.

"Time to race, George," said Marbury. "Are you ready?"

"Yassuh, I tink so," mumbled George, rubbing the sleep from his eyes.

"Today might be the best day of your life, George," said Marbury.

"Suh?"

"Mr. Foster here and I have a thousand dollars bet on Lucy, at pretty good odds. If she wins, we both stand to make a small fortune. And you'll be a free man."

"Suh?" George still didn't understand.

"You win this race, George," said Marbury, "and I'll give you your freedom."

Now George was wide awake. "You mean, if'n I win this heah race, I'se free?"

"A free man," said Marbury. "Now, come on. I don't want

to lose by default because we didn't show."

When they reached the starting line, Maguire was waiting for them.

"I didn't think you'd show up," he said. "'Course, might as well not have. No way that old bobtailed nag can take my bay, here."

"We'll see," said Marbury. "In fact, I have another five hundred dollars says we'll win. My five hundred against your bay?"

"What?" asked Maguire.

"If your bay wins, I pay you another five hundred dollars. If my horse wins, I get the bay."

A grin spread across Maguire's face.

"You're on."

As the two horses lined up for the start, sweat began to dribble down George's back. If old Lucy won this race, he'd be a free man! He was so engrossed in the thought that when the starter dropped the flag, he hesitated a moment, then realized: the race was on! He gave Lucy a dig in her side with his heels, and they were off.

The bay had gotten a big jump on them and was a good fifty yards in front. George kept kicking Lucy in the ribs, but the bay continued to pull away. One mile, two miles—three more to go, and they were now several hundred yards behind. George had to try something different.

He bent his head down low over Lucy's neck, as close to her ear as he could get.

"You a great horse," he whispered. "You bettah dan dat ol' stupid bay. You a champeen."

Lucy rolled her eyes back as if to see who it was whispering this sweet talk in her ear—but she never broke stride.

"You da greatest horse ever run," George said, louder now. "Ain't no horse ever run who was bettah dan you."

16

Lucy laid her ears back, as though to better hear what this person on her back was saying to her. George felt a subtle change in the steed underneath him, the flexing of muscles.

"Look at dat ol' dumb horse up dere. He tink he bettah dan you. He ain't bettah dan you. You da best. All you got to do is be da horse I know you is. Run up dere and catch dat sons-a-bitch!"

Now George was yelling directly into Lucy's ear.

Without any notice, Lucy suddenly exploded, nearly causing George to fall off. Five yards, ten yards—slowly but surely she closed the gap between herself and the bay.

One mile to go. George was yelling and screaming like a wild man. Lucy was flying, ears pinned back, her eyes about to pop out of her head.

They were two lengths behind the bay, now. But the finish line lay right ahead. Above his own screaming, George heard the spectators shouting, urging on whichever horse they had bet on.

With one final, mighty leap, Lucy threw herself across the line, a nose in front of the bay. A shout swelled up from the crowd. George raised one of his arms over his head in a gesture of triumph. He would have raised both, but Lucy was still running so fast he was forced to hold on with the other hand or risk falling off.

Finally, he slowed Lucy down, turned her around, and let the exhausted beast trot slowly back to where Mr. Marbury and Mr. Foster waited, the smiles on their faces stretching from ear to ear.

"You did it!" shouted Marbury, as George jumped down from Lucy's back.

"*She* did it, suh," said George. "Nevah saw a horse all a sudden start to run like she done."

"I believe you *both* did it," said Mr. Foster.

17

"Here," said Marbury. He handed George a sheet of paper. "You're free. What are you going to do now?"

"I reckon I'll head up nawth, suh, see if'n I can find a job."

"This might help," said Marbury, handing George a five-dollar gold piece.

George stared at the coin, the first one he had ever held in his hand.

"And," Marbury continued. "One more thing." He handed George the halters for both Lucy and the bay. "Here. You can have the horses, too. Do whatever you want with them. Sell them. Or maybe race them. Although . . ." he hesitated, as he looked at Lucy, ". . . I have a feeling maybe today was Lucy's one lifetime race. Whatever, the horses are yours. You did a good job today, son."

∞

"And then what happened, Papaw?"

George opened his eyes. He'd almost forgotten about the children.

"Then?" said George. "Then I headed up nawth with Lucy and the bay. I started racin' the bay at county fairs and, son of a gun, that old boy could run! I made a lot of money with him."

"And, then," interrupted Dolores, who had joined the children on the porch swing, "your great-grandpa went and got himself an education. Went to school and got a high school diploma, married your great-grandma, had eight children, including Mama Jean, and eventually sent them all off to college."

"But what about Lucy?" asked Ethel.

"Lucy never raced again. But a year later she gave birth to a foal from da bay. Gingerbread Lady is da latest in Lucy's line.

18

And, like Lucy, she jus' a ol' bobtailed nag, too. But also . . ." George grinned, ". . . like Lucy, she can still outrun any of dose utha twenty thoroughbreds we got in da stables back dere."

He gestured toward the huge barn set back some fifty yards from the house.

"Can we go out now and ride Gingerbread Lady?" asked Howard.

"I'll take them out," said Dolores.

George watched as they made their way to the barn, then leaned back against the rocker and closed his eyes. He could still feel Lucy under him, the powerful surge of her muscles, the veins popping out on her neck, her ears pinned back, eyes bulging, running for all she was worth.

*That* was the day.

The day Lucy became a champion—and he became a free man.

\*\*\*\*\*\*\*\*\*\*\*\*\*\*\*\*\*\*\*\*\*\*\*\*\*\*\*\*\*\*\*\*\*\*\*\*\*\*\*\*\*\*\*\*\*\*\*\*\*\*\*\*\*\*\*\*\*\*\*\*\*\*\*\*\*\*\*\*

Stephen C. Foster composed "Gwine to Run All Night, or De Camptown Races" in 1850.

# AFTER THE BATTLE
## 1863

It was dark, and Roo could barely see through the thick underbrush. Overhead, a canopy of hickory and elm shut out the light from the moon that hung suspended like a giant pendant against the deep velvet sky. The air, damp and cool, was a welcome relief from the scorching July day just passed. The earth felt moist and deep beneath his bare feet. He shifted his leg to convince himself it was all right. He would make it. He'd make it back, by God! He'd not come this far to end up in some damned Yankee prison!

It was time for him to move again. He rose, swayed momentarily, then gingerly ventured a step. The leg felt stiff and somewhat disassociated from the rest of his body, but in a few moments, it was forgotten in the struggle to make his way through the groping vines that grabbed at his ankles. He cursed silently to himself.

An hour later he came to the edge of the woods and stopped in the shadow of a huge tree that hovered like a silent sentry to the field spread out before him, a sea of silver, cloaked in a mantle of moonlight. Rolling hills spread out to his left, and to the right the field opened to a valley that extended as far as he could see. Cautiously, he stepped from the shadow and headed south. Not only would the hills afford more cover, but they also offered the shortest route to Tennessee.

He'd be happy enough when he was out of Kentucky. Although full of Southern sympathizers, it was still a Union state. If he ran into anyone, there'd be no way to know on which side their loyalty might lie until it was too late.

With the going easier now, the dull pain returned to his leg, and he felt an aching sensation in his gut that hadn't known any nourishment in the last two days but berries and nuts, and one piece of wormy hardtack.

The wooden canteen at his side was almost empty. He was determined to save what little water he had until he found a stream where he could refill it.

Emptier than the canteen was the worn leather cartridge box. He'd used his last cartridge in the charge on Cemetery Ridge and was fortunate to make it back to the lines with no more than a gash in his knee from some damned Yankee's bayonet.

The battle had been terrible, the fighting heavy for two days. The third day they'd huddled in the woods, waiting, while the heavy guns bombarded the Union positions. About three o'clock the order was passed to deploy and as they emerged from the woods they saw the Yanks watching them from their positions about a mile away. He'd heard Pickett had fifteen thousand men under his command for this charge, and he didn't doubt it. The long gray line extended more than half a mile and they stood man to man, rank to rank.

They'd advanced but a few hundred yards when a sheet of fire hit them. Momentarily blinded in one eye, he wiped his face on his sleeve and saw it was covered with blood: not his, but that of the men exploding around him. He hadn't been hit. Everywhere, men fell and died, but in the unexplainable fear that sometimes makes men charge ahead instead of turning

21

back, the lines kept moving forward. Then, in an instant, it all changed, and he was half conscious of men stumbling, others running past him to the shelter of the woods. He fired as fast as he could get his musket reloaded. A shrill animal yell rose from deep inside him, erupting from his throat. He found himself on the slope of the ridge. He had reached the crest and put his hand into the box by his side for another cartridge when he saw the blue-coated figure coming at him. Fingers searched frantically for a ball but found none. The Yankee thrust the bayonet deep into his leg, and he crumpled, falling and rolling back down the hill that a few minutes earlier he'd desperately fought his way up. Back in the woods, he collapsed in pain and anger.

The next day—the fourth of July—the two armies watched each other, both too exhausted and shocked from the previous day's terrible conflict to spill any more blood. He'd overheard one officer say they had suffered over twenty thousand casualties in three days.

Gettysburg was the end of the war for a lot of men.

*****

Roo put his hand to his beard, still caked with blood; there'd been no time to wipe it away. Perhaps when he reached the hills and a stream, he could stop and wash. He could wash the blood and dirt away, but there was no way he'd be able to wash from his mind the memories of that day.

He jerked erect, listening. Had he heard something or only sensed it? He'd come to the end of the field and was looking into a line of trees that spread out above him, up the hillside. He squinted his eyes as if by doing so he might look deep into the black void. Now he knew what he'd heard: running water! He plunged into the darkness, sprinting, falling, getting up again, oblivious to the throbbing in his leg. Too late, he felt the ground disappear beneath his feet. As he tumbled down the steep bank, the branches reached out to grab and hold him in a vain attempt to stop his headlong plunge.

He felt the sudden impact of his head against a rock. One naked foot went cold and wet. Then—nothing.

*****

Olivia sat for a long time, staring at the haggard figure lying on the wooden planked floor. The dirty, torn, butternut-colored shirt and pants marked him as a Reb, although she hadn't noticed any insignia. She could tell even through the blood-caked beard, he must be at least forty years old. What puzzled her most was the man's belt buckle. It had a large "U.S." on it, but he was wearing it upside down on his brown leather belt.

She and Owen found him at the riverbank, one foolish foot sticking into the water. Half dragging, half carrying him, they got him back to the house. Through it all, he remained lifeless. Though he weighed less than one-hundred-and-twenty pounds, it was all dead weight. The effort left her exhausted and trembling.

The soft pad of feet startled her. She looked and saw Owen coming through the open door, carrying the bucket of water for which they had originally gone.

"Owen, fetch that bucket over here, son, and bring me one of them there rags as you come."

She dipped the rag into the clear, cold water and gently wiped the black powder and matted blood from the man's gaunt face. Roo stirred, his cracked lips parting in a vain effort to speak.

"Hush, hush," she said softly, as she lightly touched the rag

23

to his mouth. "There'll be a time to talk, and then you can tell me."

His gray-green eyes looked confused and afraid.

"You're all right. Take a little drink of this water, whilst I clean some of this dirt off'n you."

Roo thought he had never tasted anything so good—never; not in his whole life. The water was like a magic potion restoring to him a new sense of awareness, revitalizing his brain until he began to realize what was happening.

"What's your name?" he asked the woman.

"Olivia—Olivia Cole," she said without stopping her task. "My boy over there—his name's Owen."

Roo hadn't noticed the boy before, now crouching silently in front of the fireplace. About ten, Roo judged him to be.

"Did you bring me here?" Roo asked Olivia.

"Yes, Owen and me did. And for not bein' much more than a bag of bones, you was a fearsome load. We tried to get you up in the loft, but we couldn't. Anyhow, it's cooler down here."

He looked around the small, dimly lit room. It reminded him of his own home: a fireplace at one end, a table and three chairs, and not much else, except for the plank floor on which he lay. Somehow, he never got around to putting a floor in his place.

"Are you a Johnny Reb?"

It was the boy who spoke.

Roo turned his head to the young figure, still crouching, but now several feet closer. He hesitated, wondering on which side the woman's and the boy's sympathies lay, then slowly nodded. He was sure the woman already knew.

"Was you in the fightin'?" the boy asked, edging closer to Roo.

Roo nodded again.

24

"Hush now, Owen," said Olivia. "The poor man's tired and hungry and hurt. You fetch some salt pork whilst I wash this cut. After we get some food in you you'll feel better," she added, turning to Roo.

*****

He did, Roo told himself after he wolfed down the meager portion the woman set before him. The warm food in his stomach, and the clean bandage on his leg, made him feel more secure and easier of mind as if a heavy burden had shifted itself somewhat from his shoulders. He shut his eyes and laid his head back. In a few moments, he slipped into a deep sleep.

*****

The afternoon was nearly spent when he felt a gentle tug on his shoulder.

"Here, I want you to eat some of this broth." The woman held the rich-smelling substance to him, and his nose sniffed involuntarily.

"My God, that smells good."

He took the bowl from her and voraciously downed its contents.

When he finished, Roo wiped his chin against his sleeve and glanced at the woman, really seeing her for the first time; slim, almost skinny, her face plain, with deep-set eyes, her hair, light brown, hung limply to her shoulders. Not pretty, she wasn't homely either. He judged her to be about thirty-years-old, although she could have been younger. Farm life was hard on a woman. He knew.

"Where's your husband?" he asked.

"Dead." The word came out like the hollow gong of a tone-

25

deaf bell. "He was with the Third Kentucky Cavalry at Shiloh."

"I'm sorry," said Roo.

He felt obliged to this woman who had taken him in, fed him, dressed his wound and, as far as he knew, not notified the Yankees of his presence.

"Can you tell me where I am?"

"Chickapea River's down yonder," she said, pointing. "That's what you done fell into when we found you. We're a couple miles outside of Camptown. Where you headin' for?"

"Tennessee."

"You're still a long way from there."

He stared at her hard. He wasn't sure she hadn't sent the boy to fetch the Yankee troops. He thought he ought to get up off his butt and get the hell of our there.

She saw the questioning look in his eyes and gently laid her small hand on his arm. "Don't fret. You're safe here. We ain't gonna turn you in. They's already been too much bloodshed. We ain't gonna help no more."

He relaxed and moved his gnarled hand to hers. She removed her hand and shifted her eyes from him.

"Tell me about yourself," she said.

"Oh, there ain't much to tell," he said, face coloring. "I was a farmer, same as you and your husband. I got a little land in Tennessee, 'nough to keep me and my family goin'. When the war come, two of my boys and me joined up with the 14th Tennessee. I didn't want to join, but the boys told me it would more than likely only be for six months, year at most. They reckoned that was all the longer it'd take us to whup the North. So I left Martha with my two girls and set out with the boys."

"Is Martha your wife?"

Roo paused a moment before answering.

"No, no, she ain't," he said. "My wife died four years ago. Martha's her sister. She's eighteen now and she's been livin'

26

with us ever since her folks got killed. She's a mighty good girl."

His words trailed off as he thought of how much Martha reminded him of his own dear wife, God rest her.

"But that's enough of me. You got any younguns besides—what's his name, Owen?"

"No," said Olivia. "Owen was my first and last. I never had no more after him. But he's a good boy. He ain't but nine, but he helps real good 'round the farm. 'Course, there ain't much farm left no more, not since his daddy went off to fight."

Both were silent for a long time, each immersed in their own thoughts.

"Well, now," she said, brightening. "You ain't told me your name. Here I know almost your whole family, but I don't even know you."

"Ruland. Ruland Cartee. But my friends call me 'Roo'."

"Ruland's an unusual name," said Olivia. "I don't know I ever heard it before."

"My ma wanted to call me Rudolph, after her daddy," Roo explained. "And my daddy wanted to call me Leland, after his daddy. Neither one would give in, so they compromised with Ruland."

"So, Mr. Cartee, feel up to movin' 'round a bit? That leg ain't gonna heal right if you lay there from now 'til doomsday."

She half rose, placed put one arm around his shoulders, and braced him with the other.

Gingerly, Roo stood, testing the weight on his leg. He was surprised at the strength in the woman's arms.

"C'mon, Mr. Cartee," she said. "Let's go outside and set for a spell. It's gettin' cooler now."

They sat on the porch for a long time, enjoying the coolness of evening coming on, and watched the sun disappear behind the mountains. They listened to the catbirds and whippoorwills vying for attention with their sweet singing. Owen chased a butterfly around the corner of the house and in a few moments came running triumphantly back, the specimen held tightly by its wings between two little fingers.

"Mr. Cartee." Her voice broke the stillness. "If you'd care to wash up some, the creek's right down back of the house. I got some pants and a shirt of my husband's you can put on. They'd be a tad big for you, but I reckon they might be a bit more comfortable. I got a extra pair of shoes of his, too."

Roo looked down at the soiled and torn shirt, the blood-stained pants ripped up one leg, his bare feet, one black with dirt, the other—the one that had been in the river—somewhat cleaner. He realized he didn't smell too good either. He couldn't remember the last time he'd had a bath.

"Yes, ma'am, I'd surely 'preciate that."

Olivia rose and disappeared into the house. Moments later she returned with the clothes. "Owen! Come here and show Mr. Cartee down to the river. You go with him case his leg gives him trouble."

A half-hour later Roo climbed back up the path to the house, his old uniform tucked under one arm. The new clothes hung loosely on him, but there was no arguing he looked and felt—and smelled—better than he had a short time before.

He sat down to the stew Olivia had waiting and took his time as he ate. Olivia and Owen ate slowly too, each one every so often glancing at him.

Olivia finally broke the silence, the words rushing out as though she'd been preparing for a long time what to say.

"Mr. Cartee, I know you're in a hurry to get home, and I know it's dangerous for you to stay here very long, but I surely feel you should stay a day or so and let your leg heal a little, or it's bound to give you trouble goin' over the mountain."

With great deliberation, Roo finished sopping his bowl

before answering.

"Ma'am, it's true I'd be in danger, but so would you and your boy. I shouldn't stay and risk gettin' us all shot."

"Nonsense!" she retorted. "Owen and me'll be all right. And he can be on the lookout for any government troops, cain't you, Owen?"

Owen nodded.

"Now, Mr. Cartee, I know you're tired and need some rest. You and Owen can sleep up in the loft. It gets cool up there when the sun goes down. And I'll see you both in the morning."

Dutifully, like two small children, Roo and Owen climbed up into the loft and lay down on the mats placed there. Roo know he should be gone right now, that it was foolish to linger here. But he *did* want to stay. He didn't know why—but he wanted to.

*****

Ker-plunk!

The pebble hit the water, causing ripples to spread out in ever-widening circles from the bulls-eye.

Earlier in the day, Roo and Owen had walked down to the river and spent the late afternoon hours on the riverbank catching fish that Olivia had later fried up into a royal feast.

In fact, thought Roo, the whole day had been peaceful, very serene. No one passed by. He'd spent the day resting, from time to time getting up to walk around, testing his leg. He and Olivia talked more about their families and him, especially, of how he longed to see his again. He wondered about his boys—whether they came through the fighting all right. Olivia told him about her parents, how they had died, and now there was only her and Owen.

Looking at her from time to time when she wasn't aware of it, he thought how much she reminded him of his wife. Olivia was younger than Caroline would have been, but he saw in her the Caroline of ten years ago.

He couldn't remember the last day that had been so pleasant.

"Mr. Cartee, can I ask you a question?"

"Sure, Owen, what is it?"

"How come you wear your belt buckle upside down?"

A blush spread over Roo's face as he recalled the circumstances of how he came to have the buckle.

"It's a Union buckle, you know," he said. "I usually wear suspenders, but in my last fight my suspenders broke and I darned near lost my britches. There was a dead Yankee laying there on the ground . . ."

Roo stopped, remembering the boy's father was a Yankee who'd been killed in action. But Owen didn't say anything, so Roo continued.

"He was dead, so I reckoned he didn't need his belt no more, at least not as bad as I did. So I took it. Lucky for me, my pants had a couple loops. I put the belt on and started fighting again."

"But why do you wear the buckle upside down?"

"Like I said, it's a Yankee buckle. Wearing it upside down shows I'm fighting for the confederacy."

His answer seemed to satisfy Owen.

The snap of a branch startled them both.

"No, don't get up."

It was Olivia.

"I thought I'd come down and set with you two for a while and cool off."

They sat for a long time, saying little, content to listen to the woods and the stream speaking to them. They watched as dragonflies skimmed over the water. A squirrel ran past, and Owen gave chase. In a moment he returned, without the squirrel, but with some golden flowers he'd found, the kind of thing that, to a boy of nine, signifies the wonders and the mysteries of life. He gave them to his mother and she returned his generosity with a kiss.

"Owen, it's gettin' late. Why don't you take these flowers on up to the house and put them in some water? Then you best get on up to bed."

Roo watched the young boy bound up the path toward the house until he disappeared out of sight. He was a good boy, thought Roo, a real good boy.

"Miss Olivia, you sure have a real fine boy there; must be a comfort to have him around."

"Yes, it surely is. After his daddy left I felt a terrible loneliness. When I got word he'd been killed, I felt like my life was over. If it weren't that I was all Owen had, I don't know what I would have done. Him and me, we jus' kept on goin'. I love that boy so much."

Through the dusk settling on them, Roo saw large tears had sprung to Olivia's eyes. Embarrassed, he quickly looked away.

"Ma'am, it's time I was leavin'. My leg feels a lot better, and if I start out now, I can get a lot of travelin' in while it's cool."

She kept her eyes staring straight ahead, toward the water. "I wish you didn't have to go," she said quietly.

"I know," he said. "But I have to."

He gently helped her to her feet and they headed back up the path, now almost hidden by the ever-spreading blackness of night. She stumbled, and he reached out to catch her.

He held her in his arms, hesitantly, fearfully. Then he tenderly kissed her and was surprised when she didn't turn away. He kissed her again, hungrily, eagerly, like a man who has been too long at war, and too long without a woman.

31

"Oh, Roo, Roo," she whispered. "It's been so long and I've . . . I've been so lonely."

He held her face between his hands, and once again he saw the tears running like tiny streams from her eyes.

She buried her face in his chest. "Will you stay with me tonight?" she asked.

"Yes," he said. "I will."

*****

The morning was still cool and fresh, for it was early, and the sun had just started to peek over the mountain. Roo stood in the doorway and stared at the parched field spread out before him. Two days ago his sole thought was to get back home, to find out if his family were all well, and then, somehow, rejoin Lee's army for that one last stand he knew must come: the final death knell of a dying South.

He still wanted to see his family again, but now—now the war did not seem all that important anymore. He'd found something new, something wonderful, something he thought he lost forever four years ago.

He picked up the canteen she'd filled for him with the cold stream water. He had adjusted the belt buckle so now the "U.S." appeared right side up. He'd change it again when he got to Tennessee. No one would know he was a Johnny Reb.

"You're leavin' now?" Her voice trembled.

"Yes, I have to go," he said. "But I'll be back."

He tenderly kissed her.

"I'll be back."

## THE LYNCHING OF MOSES MORGAN
## 1869

I always thought of my grandfather as a kind, loving person. My first memory of him was when I was no more than four years old. The two of us were walking in the woods behind Grandpa's farm when we came across a fawn with a broken leg. Grandpa gently picked up the frightened, shaking animal in his arms, and carried it back to the house, where he set its leg.

Over the next two months, he coddled that fawn as if it were his own child. When the leg healed, he and I led the animal out into the woods and released it. When I looked at Grandpa I was surprised to see tears running down his cheeks.

That's why it was such a shock when I started going through my grandmother's belongings after she died.

Grandpa passed away in 1932 and my grandmother continued to live alone in the small cabin they'd bought out on the banks of the Chickapea River after they'd gotten too old to run the farm anymore. By themselves, they'd packed up over sixty years of married life into the old farm wagon and moved ten miles down the road to their new home.

What few pieces of furniture they took with them—including the four-poster bed in which my father came into the world—my dad and I moved. But all the rest—the clothes, the

33

linens, the boxes of pictures, and papers, and keepsakes—everything else, they'd insisted on taking themselves.

Three years after they moved, my grandfather died. Five years later, my parents drowned in the big flood of 1937. A month ago it was Grandma's turn. Since I was an only child, as my father had been, I was the last of the line, except for my children, so it fell to me to handle the estate.

My wife, Emily, and I spent days going through the accumulation of "stuff."

"You know what I've learned from this?" she asked. Without waiting for my response she went on. "Get rid of 'stuff.' I don't want our children to have to go through this."

Emily's parents, both of whom suffered from tuberculosis, died in sanitariums, leaving little behind.

"I agree," I said. "When we've finished sorting through all of this, we're going to go through our own stuff and throw all the junk away."

It was in a small cardboard box in a closet in the pantry where I found it: what at first I thought to be merely an old, worn, white sheet. When I removed it from the box and held it up my mouth fell open. It was a Klan robe! Beneath it rested the hood, pointed and with two eye holes.

"Emily! Come here!" I shouted.

When Emily rushed into the room, she had the same dumbfounded look on her face I knew had been on mine moments earlier.

"Is that what I think it is?" she whispered.

"Sure as hell is—a Klan robe; and a hood."

"Is it your . . . ?"

"Grandpa's? Who else? Why would he have someone else's Klan robe?"

"The question is," said Emily, coming closer and touching her finger to the fabric, pulling it back quickly as though it

34

might, in some way, contaminate her, "why would your *grandfather* have one."

A good question. One I didn't have the answer to.

I knew the Klan was still active in Chickapea County, although in a clandestine way. They didn't have public demonstrations as they'd had ten or fifteen years earlier. Still, everyone knew they were there, and a lot of people, even the ones who weren't Klansmen, knew who they were.

But my grandfather? I couldn't believe it!

I laid the robe aside and placed the hood on top of it. At the bottom of the box was an envelope. When I picked it up the contents came tumbling out: four yellowed news clippings, all from the front page of the *Camptown Southern Gazette*.

I read the headline of the first one.

### MOSES MORGAN LYNCHED BY KLAN! WIFE BEATEN TO DEATH.

I motioned Emily to sit down on the stool next to me and began to read out loud.

*Moses Morgan, a nigger well known in these parts, was lynched in his front yard yesterday by a cowardly mob of Klansmen.*

*According to an anonymous source, Morgan had been accused by one of the Klansmen of stealing onto his property in the dead of night and carrying off one of his prize sows.*

*Although a thorough search of Morgan's place failed to turn up any sign of the sow, the aggrieved party swore he'd recognized Morgan as he made his getaway through the woods, since Morgan once worked for him as a field hand. That apparently was enough for the mob, as they dragged the nigger to a tall sycamore tree in the front yard of his home and strung him up while his wife and three little children looked on.*

*Morgan's wife tried to stop the hanging, but was restrained by the Klansmen.*

*Following the lynching, Mrs. Morgan begged the Klansmen to allow her to go into the house to get a blanket to wrap her husband up in in order to bury him. When she returned, however, she had a shotgun, which she fired into the crowd of Klansmen, killing two and seriously wounding three others.*

*Before she could reload, she was grabbed and knocked to the ground, where she was beaten to death. In the confusion the three young children ran into the woods. Their whereabouts is still unknown.*

*Sheriff Tree Lancaster says he is investigating the incident.*

"My God," said Emily.

I looked at the date on the masthead: August 4th, 1869. Seventy years ago.

I picked up the second clipping and saw it was dated three days later. Its headline read:

## KLANSMEN ARRESTED IN MORGAN LYNCHING

*Sheriff Lancaster announced today that an arrest has been made in the lynching this past Tuesday of Moses Morgan. Mr. Morgan was killed in his front yard while his wife and three children looked on. Mrs. Morgan was beaten to death by the Klansmen after she fired a shotgun at them, killing two and wounding three others. The dead were identified by Dr. Jacobson, the County Coroner as Herman Whiting and Lester Bennefield. The three men who were injured were identified as Oren Adamson, Wimpy Trinkle, and Clarence Jones.*

*In addition to the five men listed above, it is believed seven others were present at the time of the crime and may have participated in the lynching. Five have been apprehended: Melvin Wolcott, Madison Wolcott, Homer Adamson, Jersey McPherson, and Liddy Shores. The identities and locations of the other two men are not known at this time. Sheriff Lancaster says the Freedmen's Bureau is assisting with the investigation.*

Wondering for a moment what the Freedmen's Bureau was, I laid the article aside and picked up the third one, dated September 14, 1869.

## KLANSMEN FOUND GUILTY
## IN MORGAN LYNCHING

*The seven known surviving Klansmen involved in the killing of Moses Morgan and his wife last month were found guilty yesterday by a jury of their peers, and Judge Wilbur Townsend sentenced each of them to be hung by the neck until dead. It is believed to be the first time in the history of Chickapea County that a white man has been found guilty of killing a nigger. It is also believed to be the largest number of defendants ever to receive the death penalty at the same time. Wimpy Trinkle, who survived the shotgun blast from Leafy Morgan's gun that killed Herman Whiting and Lester Bennefield instantly, died a week following the incident.*

*Judge Townsend instructed Sheriff Lancaster to have seven gallows constructed by this coming Saturday, the date set for the execution.*

*The main evidence against the culprits came from the three surviving Morgan children, who were found hiding in the woods, and from an unknown eyewitness, said to be a white man. None of the witnesses appeared in court, the niggers not being able to legally, and the white man apparently fearing for his life. Judge Townsend said he spoke to all four in private, and was convinced their testimony, which he conveyed to the jury, was true.*

*The other two suspected Klansmen reported to be at the lynching have still not been identified.*

I picked up the final clipping.

## KLANSMEN EXECUTED

*The populace of Camptown was treated to a rare sight this past Saturday, when seven men were hung one by one in the town square.*

*Reporters from all over came to witness what many said could never happen in Kentucky: white men being executed for killing a nigger. The wives and children of the doomed men presented a pitiful sight as they wept for their husbands and fathers and sons.*

*Sheriff Lancaster prohibited any niggers from being present, fearing their presence might start a riot among those whites who were opposed to the sentence. The lone exception was the Reverend Fulton Glover, who was there representing the Freedmen's Bureau.*

*When asked the status of the search for the two remaining killers, the sheriff said there were no leads and in all likelihood their identities would remain a mystery.*

"Are you thinking what I'm thinking?" asked Emily.

I nodded. "That my grandfather might have been one of the two who were never found."

That's when it hit me.

"The names," I said. "I've seen those names before!"

"Where?"

I wrinkled my brow. Where? Where had I seen them? Then I remembered.

"On a picture; a photograph my grandparents had hanging on a wall in the attic at their old farmhouse."

"I wonder if they kept it;" said Emily, "if it's still here someplace."

"We're sure as hell going to find out," I said. "Come on."

For the next two hours, we searched every square inch of the little cabin, going through every box, every trunk. Then I found the picture, neatly laid between some of Grandmother's good linens, the ones she only used for company, when they used to have company.

"Emily! I've got it! Here it is!"

Emily came running from the kitchen, where she'd been searching through my grandmother's recipes.

"Look!" I said. "I knew I remembered right. See, there are twelve men in the photograph, and a name is written under each of them."

Looking to find my grandfather's name and picture, I spotted him, second from the left in the top row. At the bottom were calligraphed the words *Exalted Order of the Knights of Adam*. I ran into the bedroom where I'd left the newspaper clippings and quickly compared names. They were all there! All the men who had been involved in the lynching were in the picture, including my grandfather and one other man: a William J. Swaney.

"This is them," I said. "These are the men who lynched Moses Morgan and were hanged."

"Except for your grandfather and this William Swaney," replied Emily.

"Except for those two. They must have been the ones who got away."

"Do you know who William Swaney is?" asked Emily.

"Never heard of him."

I turned the picture over. On the back was written: *Billy knows the truth.*

"Look at this," I said.

Emily read it. "Billy knows the truth? What does that mean? What truth? And who's Billy?"

"I don't know what the truth is. But I'd bet Billy is William J. Swaney. Get your coat."

"Where we going?"

"Into town. We're going to see if we can find anyone who ever heard of William Swaney."

Our first stop was the Post Office. Ever since I could remember, Mrs. Winetropp had run Camptown's little post office out of the front of the feed and grain store she and her husband owned. I figured if anybody would know "Billy," she would.

"Billy Swaney? Why, yes, I remember him; haven't seen him in a coon's age, though. Believe he moved a couple of years back to be with his sister somewhere up in Indiana."

"Do you know his sister's name?" I asked.

Mrs. Winetropp shook her head. "I was only a girl when she left town. Know she got married, but I have no idea who to."

I pursed my lips. How could I find him now?

"'Course, that ain't the end of it," came a voice from the back of the store.

Mr. Winetropp came hobbling out.

"What do you mean?" asked Mrs. Winetropp.

"Saw Billy Swaney last month over in Crownsville when I drove over to drop off an order to Mrs. Schutte. He's living there now, boarding at her place. Seems his sister died last year, and Billy wanted to come back home. But for some reason, he didn't want to come back to Camptown. He didn't say why and I didn't ask."

"He's there now?" I asked, optimism framing my words.

"Unless he's done gone and died," said Mr. Winetropp.

I got the directions to Mrs. Schutte's boarding house and hurried Emily out to the car.

"Come on," I said, "we're going to Crownsville."

*****

"William Swaney?"

I'm not sure what I expected, but certainly not the shriveled-up little man sitting in the rocking chair before me.

"That be me, son. What can I do fer you?"

Without answering, I handed him the picture.

He took it, studied it for a moment, and then his eyes lit up.

"My Lawd! I hain't seen this pitcher fer—what? Sixty years! More'n that, maybe. Where'd you git this pitcher, son?"

"So you are the William Swaney in the picture?" I asked, ignoring his question.

"'Course I am. How come you ask? Who are you? How'd you come by this here pitcher?"

"I'm Obadiah McCormick's grandson," I said.

"Lawdy be! Obadiah's grandson! Now, I'll be switched. Heard he passed away some years back; my condolences."

I took the picture from his hands and flipped it over.

"And are you the Billy that 'knows the truth'?"

The old man looked perplexed. "What truth?"

"My guess," I said as evenly as I could, "would be the truth about the lynching of Moses Morgan."

The color drained from the old man's face, and he seemed to go limp.

"What do you know about that?" he whispered.

I handed him the newspaper clippings. "About everything there is to know."

I waited while he read through the clippings. When he finally looked up, I said, "You and my grandfather are the two men they never caught, aren't you?"

The old man nodded.

"And was it one of you who gave the sheriff the names of the other men who'd taken part in the lynching?"

"Your grandpop," said Swaney.

"Why didn't the other seven men turn you two in?" I asked.

"The code, I reckon. Klansmen didn't rat on other Klansmen."

"And yet my grandfather did."

"It's obvious you don't know the *whole* story then, son," said Swaney.

"What do you mean?"

"I mean, me and your grandpop, we weren't really Klansmen."

"What do you mean 'you weren't really Klansmen'? Right there both of you are in the picture with the other sons-a-bitches! And you as good as admitted you'd been there that day when they lynched that poor bastard and beat his wife to death."

"That's all true. But, like the back of the pitcher says, I know the truth."

"And what might that be?" I asked, by now finding it hard to accept any kind of excuse this old man might offer.

"Me and your grandpop, we tried to stop the lynching—and the beating that poor old woman took."

"I don't believe you! Why would you try to stop it if you were a part of it?"

"That's just it. We wasn't a part of it. That is, we wasn't *really* Klansmen—well, not in our hearts, anyways."

"What are you saying?"

"You ever heard of the Freedmen's Bureau?"

My mind registered the two references in the newspaper clippings.

"Two of these articles mentioned some such organization I've never heard of. What about it?"

"The Freedmen's Bureau was set up by the federal guvamint at the end of the war—that'd be the one between the

42

states. The Bureau was set up to help Negroes get land and fair trials, and . . . well, just a fair shake all around."

"What's does that have to do with this?" I was quickly becoming agitated.

"Your grandpop and me—we worked for the Freedmen's Bureau."

"You 'worked' for it?"

"We was what you'd call 'secret agents'—spies, so to speak."

"Secret agents? Spies?"

"That's right. When the guvamint found out the Klan was organizin' a group here in Chickapea County, one of their men went to your grandpop and asked him to get into it, so's he could keep an eye on what they was a'doin' and report back. That feller knew which way your grandpop's loyalties lay. And he knew your grandpop carried a lot of influence. If he said he wanted to join the Klan, they'd snatch him up in a minute. Your grandpop got in, and he recruited me to partner with him.

"That night, we all headed out to old Moses Morgan's place to get Liddy Shores's sow back. Your grandpop and I, we thought, yeah, the old Negro stold it. But when we couldn't find hide nor hair of that damn pig—sorry, ma'am—that pig anywheres on Morgan's place, we knew he hadn't done it. But old Liddy, he didn't care. In fact, I think he made up the whole story so's he'd have an excuse to lynch old Morgan. You know, there was bad blood between them two anyways, from when Moses worked for him on his farm.

"Well, when Liddy got those other Klansmen riled up enough they wanta to string old Moses up, me and your grandpop did our best to talk them out of it. Went so far as to threaten Liddy if he let it happen.

"But by this time, they was all way past listenin'. Four of

43

them held me and your grandpop down, whilst another four took old Moses and hung him from that there sycamore. He didn't go easy, though, a fightin' them all the way. And poor old Mrs. Morgan, she was a cryin' and wailin' whilst two of the fellers held her back.

"After old Moses quit a twitchin', Mrs. Morgan asked if she couldn't go back in the house to get somethin' to wrap her husband's body in. I seed she'd calmed down considerable by then. In fact, she was *real* calm.

"All of a sudden she comes a blastin' with a shotgun out of her cabin, and Liddy and Melvin—I think it was Melvin, it was a long time ago—anyways, they started beatin' on her. Me and your grandpop tried to stop that, too, but Madison—that'd be Melvin's brother—pulled a gun on us and told us he'd just as soon shoot our ass as look at us—sorry again, ma'am. Weren't nothin' we could do. When they finally quit beatin' on that poor old nigger, she was dead.

"They went to check on the other fellers, and found two of them dead, and three of them wounded. Can you believe it? They hated that old woman so much they took the time to beat her to death 'fore they looked to see how their friends was a'doin'!"

I was fascinated by what the old man was saying. "Did the families of those other Klansmen know my grandfather turned them in?" I asked. "And did they ever find out about the two of you working for the Freedmen's Bureau?"

"I'm purty sure they never knowed who it was snitched on them. They'd never have figgered a fellow Klansman could do that. So, no, I don't guess they ever connected us with the Bureau, either. But I weren't sure. That's why I left Kentucky and moved up to Indianapolis."

"But now you're back."

"Yep, my sister died and, besides, when I die I want it to be here in Kentucky. But I didn't feel right easy going back to Camptown. That's why I moved here to Crownsville."

After I thanked Billy for his time, Emily and I made our way back to the car.

Emily put her hand in mine.

"So your grandfather was a hero," she said, as we started our trip back to Camptown.

"I guess he was," I said. "I guess he was."

I'll never know why my grandfather kept the robe and hood, and that photograph. But I'm glad now he did. Otherwise, as Emily said, I would never have known how much of a hero he really was.

We kept everything, too, including the newspaper clippings, so our children, and our grandchildren, would know—as I had always known—what a good, kind, loving man my grandfather truly was.

# THE DAY I WHIPPED JOHN L. SULLIVAN
## 1880

I was always big for my age.

Mama said when I was born I weighed eleven pounds, fourteen ounces. Said I darned near killed her coming out.

By the time I was ten I was up to a hundred and fifty pounds. At age twenty I weighed over two-fifty, 'cordin' to the scale at Mr. Mullaney's feed and grain store.

Now Pa weren't no slouch himself. He must have weighed two hundred and ten pounds if he weighed an ounce. Mama, on the other hand, was only 'bout half as big as Pa, if that.

One good thing about being so big: nobody ever messed with me. All through school—the eighth grade being as far as I went since after that I had to work full time on the farm—I was known as "Big Hank."

One of my favorite things in all the world was rasslin'. There weren't nobody for eight or ten counties 'round could beat me at it. One time this big feller from over to Bourbon County came by. He'd heard about me, and figgered he could take me. Heck, weren't no contest at all. I pinned him in about thirty seconds. After that, there weren't too many others who reckoned they might whip me.

'Course, a bad thing about being so big was, none of the girls liked me. Leastways, I don't think they did. For instance, whenever there was a barn dance out at Colonel Alamander's place, I went. But every time I asked a girl to dance she always had a reason why she didn't want to.

After a while, I quit going to the dances. I stayed home and worked the farm and, ever once in a while, found somebody willing to rassle me.

Oh, and read. I loved to read.

Miss Claiborne, the teacher at the school, had been real sorry to hear I wasn't coming back after the eighth grade, 'cause she thought I was smart enough to finish school and maybe make something of myself. Leastways, that's what she told me.

To make up for my lack of continuin' education, she'd stop by the house every coupla weeks and leave me a book to read. My all-time favorites were *The Adventures of Tom Sawyer* and *The Last of the Mohicans*.

When I was fifteen, I discovered the *Camptown Southern Gazette*.

Up 'til then, what little I knew about life outside of Chickapea County, Kentucky, was what I picked up from runnin' errands for Miss Claiborne's daddy, who owned the hotel. I tried to be around whenever a coach'd come into town, so's I could eavesdrop on whatever was being said.

The *Gazette* opened up a whole new world for me.

The first story I remember that made an impression on me was about a new horse race up in Louisville, called the Kentucky Derby, won by some horse named Aristides—or Aristotle, or something like that.

The next year, in 1876, there was a big article about an exposition in Philadelphia, where some feller showed off an invention called the "telephone."

Yes, sir, there definitely was more to life than Chickapea County, Kentucky.

Now, while my passion was rasslin', my pa's was prize fightin'. Not that he personally participated—my ma wouldn't let him. Said if he got beat up, who'd work the farm? Not her, by Jiminy! she said. But she let him go watch.

Whenever Pa heard a prizefight was being held somewhere close by he'd jump on our plow horse, old Sketchem, and ride over to where it was happening, as far as Lexington, sometimes.

When I was sixteen, Pa took me with him up to Cincinnati to buy a new bull, ours having keeled over from old age. On the way back we stopped at a saloon in Covington. While Pa was having his usual beer and me my sarsaparilla, we overhead two fellers at the bar talking about a prizefight that was to take place the next day. No way Pa was going to let the chance to see a prizefight go by, so he inquired where the fight was gonna happen. After we left the saloon we headed for the place where the fight was going to take place and bedded down there for the night, sleeping in the wagon.

One of the fighters was named Joe Goss. The other was Tom Allen. Neither of them was spring chickens. I reckoned each must have been in their late thirties or early forties. I remember Goss best, mostly because he was a short fellow, no more than five-foot-eight, and I knowed he couldn't have weighed more than a hundred and seventy-five pounds, most of it fat—not that Allen was in any better shape.

But more than that, I remember how he won the fight when Allen was disqualified in the twenty-second round for hitting him while he knelt on the grass after being knocked down. That was my first prizefight.

In the next week's edition of the *Gazette,* I saw a small article on the back page about the fight that quoted Goss claiming the title of "American Champion."

After that, I watched for any stories the *Gazette* might run about prizefighting. There weren't many, as the sport didn't have a good reputation, but ever once in a while, I'd find one.

In April of 1880, four years after watching my first prizefight, I saw an article in the *Gazette*, picked up from the *Boston Daily Globe*, 'bout a three-round exhibition held there between Joe Goss and some young feller named John Sullivan. Goss was still considered the "American Champion," as a result of his "win" over Tom Allen in 1876. The article indicated, though, he'd been badly beaten by the newcomer, Sullivan.

Three months later I spotted another story about John Sullivan, again picked up by the *Gazette* from the *Globe*. This time Sullivan had beat up on some hapless fellow by the name of George Rooke, with the fight again only lasting three rounds, like the one with Goss had. The paper referred to Sullivan as the "Highland Boy." Why, I don't know.

Two days before Christmas I was sweepin' the floor at the hotel when the stage arrived and a young feller, dressed like a dandy, stepped off. While Mr. Claiborne was takin' down some information, I overheard the man tell him he was from Boston and he was in town to visit an aunt who lived here, but he'd only be staying for a few days since he'd heard an old friend of his, John Sullivan, was going to be in a prizefight in Cincinnati. My ears pricked up!

Seems Sullivan had had an exhibition bout with some fighter two days earlier in which he'd pounded his opponent all over the ring. The loser claimed afterward he'd been ill, and demanded a real fight, so one was scheduled for Christmas Eve.

Christmas Eve! There was no way Ma would let Pa and me get away on Christmas Eve for a prizefight. For sure, we'd be spendin' the evenin' in church. I decided to not even mention the fight to Pa.

Christmas fell on a Saturday that year. Although it was a holiday, the Tipsy Toad Saloon was open for business as usual, in spite of the law saying it couldn't be. Sheriff Lancaster merely looked the other way.

Ma didn't allow any work on Christmas, and since things were kind of dull around the farm 'bout three in the afternoon I'd gone into town to see if anything was stirring. When I arrived at the hotel—I figgered if anything *was* goin' on, it'd be the place to find out—the lobby was a hubbub of activity.

"What's happenin'?" I asked Mr. Claiborne, who owned the hotel.

"You ain't heard?" he answered.

"Heard what?"

"That there feller who fought that fight up there in Cincinnati last night? He's in town! Over at the Tipsy Toad!"

"John Sullivan?"

"That's right! Seems he beat the feller again; this time in seven rounds."

"But . . . why's he here—in Camptown?"

"You remember the dandy who was in a couple days ago, said he was a friend of Sullivan's? 'Pears he was tellin' the truth. Talked him into comin' down here to his aunt's for Christmas. 'Course I don't reckon they spent much time at the aunt's. Been over at the Tipsy Toad since early this mornin', drinkin' and laughin', and carryin' on."

John Sullivan! Here in Camptown! I had to see this for myself.

When I got to the saloon, the place was packed. But it was easy to spot the man of the hour. He stood at the bar, a broad smile on his face, a drink in one hand and a cigar in the other, surrounded by an admirin' throng of men along with a few of the town's more disreputable women. You know the kind I mean.

I was struck by the fact that, unlike the two fighters I'd seen up in Boone County some four years earlier, he was neither old nor out of shape. In fact, he appeared to be not much older than me. And, while not nearly as big as me, I guessed him to weigh right around two hundred pounds, most of which, I could tell, even from the jacket coat he wore, was muscle. His hair was close-cropped and he was clean-shaven, not having yet grown the mustache that identified him so much in later years. He must not have been hit all that much in any of his fights, since his face still had a youngish look, with no cuts or scars.

A man standin' next to me grabbed my arm and, pullin' me behind him, pushed his way through the crowd until we stood directly in front of Sullivan

"Here he is!" the old man yelled out, trying to be heard above the roar of the crowd. "Here's the one we was tellin' you about."

Sullivan turned away from the young girl whispering in his ear and looked up at me—something I'm sure he didn't do too often, since he stood almost six feet, taller than most of his opponents, but still some three inches shorter than me.

For a few minutes, he studied me up and down, then smiled and said, "They say you can beat me in a match."

For a moment I stood there, speechless. Me? Fight John Sullivan? I'd never had a fight in my life! And he was a professional!

"Uh, Mr. Sullivan," I managed to get out, "these fellers been telling you a lie. I ain't no fighter. I ain't never been in a fight in my life . . . 'cept that one time in the sixth grade, when Scooter McBain tried to take my lunch, and I stopped him. No sir, I ain't no prizefighter like you."

"I don't think they were talking about a prizefight. They said you were a pretty good wrestler."

It took a few moments for what he'd said to sink in. But then I started to understand.

"You sayin' you want to rassle me?" I asked, dumbfounded.

"That's right," said Sullivan.

"I don't know," I said, shaking my head.

"I'm putting up five dollars as part of the purse, and the other gents here have offered to match it. Winner take all."

Ten dollars! Now you may think ten dollars ain't much, but believe me, in 1880 it was a heck of a lot of money—especially for a farm boy like me.

"Wait a minute," I said. "How much do I have to put up?"

"Not a red cent," said Sullivan.

"And what do the other fellers get out of it that're puttin' up their money?"

Mr. Sullivan smiled. "Why, they get to watch me whip your butt—unless you should whip mine; which ain't likely."

How could I pass it up?

"Okay," I said. "When and where?"

"My barn!" shouted Mr. Mullaney. "There's plenty of hay on the floor and plenty of room for looking on. 'Sides, it's warm in there. Let's go!"

"Right now?" I asked.

"Why not?" answered Sullivan.

By the time we reached the barn, there must have been twenty or thirty men tagging along, as word got out pretty fast about what was about to happen. The women from the saloon were told they weren't welcome—wasn't a proper thing for them to be watching two half-naked men rollin' 'round on the ground.

Mr. Sullivan had changed into the tights he wore when he boxed, and taken off his shirt, to reveal the most muscular body I'd ever seen. I still had on the overalls I'd worn into town, but I took my shirt off, too. I didn't find the barn

52

nowhere near as warm as Mr. Mullaney made it sound, but I figgered in a few minutes I'd be sweatin' up plenty from rasslin'.

Judge Townsend offered to serve as the referee for what few rules there were: no eye-gouging, no kneeing the groin—things like that. There wouldn't be any rounds: we'd just rassle 'til one of us pinned the other for a count of three, or one of us gave up. I knew for sure it wouldn't be me.

As soon as we came together Mr. Sullivan got me in a bear hug—which wasn't easy, considering how big around my waist is. I know he was surprised when I slipped my arms under his and broke free, in the process knockin' him back against the wall.

Then he came after me with a vengeance.

For the next hour, we rassled back and forth, first him gettin' an advantage, then me. By that time both of us was breathin' pretty hard. But neither of us could keep the other pinned long enough for Judge Townsend to count to three.

Then, Mr. Sullivan made a mistake. I got him on his back, sittin' on him, facin' his legs, with my legs pinnin' his arms, and my butt practically in his face. I grabbed his wrists with my hands, and pinned them to the floor, all the time avoidin' his legs, which he tried to wrap around my head.

When I heard the judge count to three and wave his arms, indicatin' the match was over, I jumped up, ready to run out the door. I was sure Mr. Sullivan was so mad he was goin' to start punchin' on me.

Instead, he got to his feet, smiled, and put out his hand.

"You beat me fair and square, boy," he said. "The purse is yours."

Everyone was yellin' and clappin'. I guess they was as happy as I was. We all moseyed back over to the Tipsy Toad and drank beer.

John Sullivan, soon to be known as John "L." Sullivan, went on to be acknowledged as the first true heavyweight boxin' champion of the world. The records show he lost only one fight in his life, to "Gentleman" Jim Corbett, on September 7th, 1892.

What they don't show, but what *I* know, as do a lot of folks in Camptown, Kentucky, is that he lost two, the first one bein' to me in a rasslin' match on Christmas Day, December 25th, 1880.

The day I whipped John L. Sullivan.

## THE POKER GAME
## 1888

I glanced out the window and seen him comin' down the street.

Through the dusk that was just beginnin' to lay down over the town, I knowed it was him from the gold vest. Most men hereabouts, them that wore vests, mostly wore black ones. Oh, sure, there was a couple who sported fancy red ones. And there was Mr. Ogleman, who owned the barbershop. He wore a purty purple one. But Preacherman was the only one who wore a gold one.

He was a sharp dresser, too. Always had on a clean, white shirt, starched so stiff, for the life of me, I don't know how he got into it; a little string tie; and a black frock coat that I knowed hid the two Colt Navy revolvers ridin' on either side of his hips.

Under the black Stetson he wore, his silver hair came tumblin' down to his shoulders.

I knowed where he was headin'. Right up here to this very room, on the second floor of the Tipsy Toad Saloon, for the weekly Friday night poker game.

I looked at the regulars, who'd already been playin' for the last hour: Miss Elly, who owned the Tipsy Toad; old Doc Jacobson, the town undertaker and county coroner; Mr. Cole, the editor of our local newspaper, *the Camptown Southern Gazette;* and Judge Townsend, who was the . . . well, he was the judge. The only one missin'—besides Preacherman—was Colonel Alamander, who owned a big farm this side of Crownsville. He'd gone off up to Lexington the day before for his sister's funeral.

But sittin' in his chair was a stranger they'd let in the game just for that night. I reckon I was downstairs gettin' beers for Mr. Jacobson and Mr. Cole when they introduced the stranger around, so I didn't get his name. That's my job, gettin' the players beer, or whiskey, or anything else they needed. My name's Andy and I work for Miss Elly.

I knowed I didn't like the stranger's looks. He was slick lookin', like the oil that comes pumpin' up out of the ground over there on Freddy Dudley's farm. And, he wore a black patch over one eye.

The air in the room was already so thick from the cigars they was all smokin'—all of 'em 'cept Miss Elly—she didn't smoke, but she chewed—you could'a cut it with a butter knife. Like I said, they'd been playin' for 'bout an hour, and it seemed the stranger was havin' an uncommon run of good luck. Seemed like he was winnin' almost every pot.

I heard Preacherman's footsteps on the wooden stairs. Just as he came through the door, Judge Townsend asked me to run down and fetch him up a whiskey, so if they introduced the stranger to Preacherman I didn't catch his name then, neither.

By the time I got back upstairs, old "One Eye"—that's what I was callin' him to myself now—was dealin' out a hand of seven-card stud. As usual, he won.

Over the next couple hours, the stranger's luck continued. I never seen nobody so lucky at cards. I mean, Preacherman, he was good, but this guy—why, he was amazin'!

I noticed whenever it was One Eye's turn to deal, Preacherman watched him real close like. Even when someone else was dealin', Preacherman seemed to take an uncommon interest in the stranger's hands.

A little after midnight I brought a tray of sandwiches up for everyone. It was Preacherman's turn to deal. He shuffled the cards once, twice—then set the deck down on the table.

"I been havin' such bum luck tonight," he said. "No one would object if I offered up a little prayer, would they?"

Of course, nobody said "no." If Preacherman wanted to pray, they wasn't about to tell him he couldn't. Old One Eye looked amused, but he didn't say nothin'.

Preacherman bowed his head and closed his eyes. Everybody else followed suit—everybody, that is, except the stranger. He just sat there, lookin' straight ahead at Preacherman, a smirk on his lips.

"Oh, Lord," Preacherman began, "this is an awful shame. But there's someone cheatin' in this here game. And it ain't gonna do for me to name the guy. But now, we all know cheatin's an awful crime, and if I find him cheatin' just one more time, I'm gonna take my fist and close that other eye. Amen."

A chorus of "amens" echoed around the table and six pairs of eyes—includin' mine—turned to look at the stranger, who had begun to sweat somethin' terrible, even though it weren't all that hot in the room.

One Eye stood and reached down to pick up his money. "It's late," he said. "I reckon I should be going."

Quicker'n a wink, six guns appeared on the table, includin' both of Preacherman's Colt revolvers, and Miss Elly's little single-shot derringer.

"No, I don't think so," said Preacherman, in a soft voice. "The evening's just gettin' started. Sit down. Whose turn is it to deal?"

The stranger sat back down. He didn't say nothin'.

"Buck's in front of me," said Mr. Cole. "Reckon it's my turn."

Over the next couple hours, the stranger's luck took a sudden turn for the worse. Where before he'd been winnin' almost every hand, now he couldn't buy a pot.

At last, he was down to his last eagle. Him and Preacherman was the only two still in, and Preacherman bet ten dollars on the three Queens and a deuce showin' in his five-card stud hand. Old One Eye had three Kings and a ten showin', but that didn't seem to faze Preacherman.

"Call," said One Eye, shovin' his eagle to the middle of the table.

"Four Queens," said Preacherman, turnin' over the fourth lady.

"Your pot," said One Eye, turnin' his four up cards over, and standin' up. He looked at Preacherman. "I reckon it's all right for me to go now, isn't it?"

"I reckon so," said Preacherman. "I assume you'll be leavin' on the mornin' stage?"

"I reckon so," said the stranger.

"Andy, you straighten up, will you?" asked Miss Elly.

"Yes, ma'am," I replied.

It only took me a few minutes to clear the glasses and plates from the table. By then, all the players were gone. Out of curiosity, I turned over One Eye's hole card. It was the fourth King! He had Preacherman beat!

"He had the best hand, didn't he?"

I spun around to see Preacherman standin' there in the doorway. I guessed he'd come back for somethin'. I nodded, dumbly.

"I knew he had the best hand," said Preacherman.

"How'd you know?" I asked.

"I dealt it to him. I knew what he had. And *he* knew *I* knew what he had."

"But . . . ?"

"Why didn't he claim the pot?"

I nodded.

"Sometimes it's better *not* to win, to just throw in your cards and leave. Even cheaters know that. You know what I mean?"

I nodded again, though I wasn't sure I *did* understand.

Preacherman flipped me a five-dollar gold piece. "Here, Andy. You did a good job tonight. See you next Friday."

"Thanks," I said.

Preacherman tipped his hat and walked out the door.

I went back to straightenin' up.

## TOM
## 1905 - 1911

Nobody ever was exactly sure how Tom came to show up in Camptown. All we knew was, one day, in the summer of 1905, there he was, strutting down Main Street like he owned the place.

Everybody stopped dead in their tracks to watch him. Mrs. McCorkle, who was coming out of the general store, was so startled she dropped the bag of apples she'd just bought, causing most of them to roll out into the street. Old Mr. Biddlemire came bouncing out of Ogleman's barber shop, his face still half-covered with shaving cream, and a hair drape—or whatever you call the thing Mr. Ogleman ties on his customers to keep from getting hair all over their clothes—flapping in the wind. Mr. Ogleman was right on his heels. They'd spotted old Tom through the window and had come outside to get a better look.

We all stared while Tom, paying nary a bit of attention to any of us, made his way down the street until he came to Mr. Mullaney's feed and grain store where he turned and disappeared down the alley that ran alongside the building.

That's when the buzzing started.

"My lands, did you ever *see* such a thing!" "Lawd, I cain't believe my eyes!" "They ain't *never* been nothin' like that here in

60

Camptown before!"

Paddy O'Brien said he was going to go get his shotgun, but cooler heads prevailed.

The next day, about the same time, Tom showed up again.

And, like the day before, he strutted down Main Street, not uttering a sound, until he came to the grain and feed store where, again, he headed down the alley. There was some talk of following old Tom, to see where he was headed, or what he was up to, but that's all it ever amounted to: talk. I won't say it was because we was all scared but, hey, he was one ferocious looking critter.

Everybody reckoned he must have been a good four feet tall, which was pretty much confirmed the third day when Tom, coming 'round the corner at the feed and grain store, came face to face, so to speak, with Miss Eunice Claiborne, who everybody knew was no more than a tad over four feet. The two of them stood there for a few seconds, eyeing one another, until Miss Claiborne swooned over in a dead faint. Old Tom, he just stepped around her and continued on his way, like Miss Claiborne's fainting was an everyday occurrence. Two or three townsfolk rushed to help revive the poor woman who, by some accounts, never fully recovered from the encounter.

Mr. Mullaney, who'd been looking out the front window of his store, and who'd gotten a good look at Tom when he walked by, said he reckoned Tom must have weighed at least forty pounds—which is mighty big for a turkey, I can tell you. Especially one that stands four feet tall.

Now we got wild turkeys here in Kentucky—plenty of them. But nothing like Old Tom.

Our turkeys never get more than about three feet tall, if that. And if you find one that weighs over twenty-five pounds why, my goodness, that little gobbler's been eating real good.

Besides, our birds are kind of plain looking—even the toms. But Old Tom, he was a—I guess the word I'm looking for is: majestic—he was a *majestic* looking turkey, with this huge fan-shaped tail that had tan and black and brown feathers, and an enormous bright red wattle, red as the cardinal who comes each afternoon at three o'clock to peck the cracked corn folks leave for him there on the little stand I put up out in front of my butcher shop. And Tom's beard—why it was so long it almost dragged the ground.

Shorty Evans, who used to live down south in Florida, thought Tom could be a Florida turkey, that he'd seen a few somewhat like him down there, though none quite so big. Nobody could figure out how Tom might have got to Kentucky from Florida—if, indeed, that was where he was from—or why he was here, but here he was, sure as shootin'.

After about a week of this ritual of Tom walking down Main Street and making his customary turn at the feed and grain store, he wasn't nearly the spectacle he'd been those first two or three days. And Miss Claiborne kept a wary eye out for him, as she had no desire to come face to face again; so, no more fainting episodes.

We'd figured out he was going behind the grain and feed store because that's where the grain wagons unloaded, and there was always some that spilled out onto the ground. Tom was having his daily lunch there.

Some nights he was spotted hanging out behind the general store. Mr. McGinnis said he figured it was because he threw the rotten apples out there. That'd be Tom's dinner.

Pretty soon, Tom became a town regular. You could almost set your watch by his daily lunch foray. He didn't bother nobody, and nobody bothered him—including all the dogs in town. They seemed to sense old Tom was nothing to be trifled with.

Young Mrs. Buhlig kinda took a liking to Tom. And he seemed to favor her, too, and her little baby boy. Whenever he spotted the two of them, he'd waddle over and sneak a peek at little Gunther in his carriage. Mrs. Buhlig always had a snack for Tom: some acorns, or fruit. She's the one who officially named him Tom; although, when you stop to think about it, what else would you call a tom turkey—Percy?

One day while Tom was taking his daily stroll down the street he happened to meet up with Ezra Limpke, who kept a place out by the Chickapea River, and his mangy hound, Jinx.

Now, Ezra wasn't the friendliest sort of fellow, nor did he care much for socializing. He only came into town when he absolutely had to, which was to buy supplies. Otherwise, he was content to keep to himself, living out there in the wilderness, him and his old dog. Like his master, Jinx weren't all that friendly, either.

In fact, when the two of them came to town, all the women made their children come inside, and all the men chained up their dogs. Otherwise, Jinx might have killed them—the dogs, that is. I'm not real sure why the women made their children come inside, 'cause I don't think Jinx would have hurt them. Or Ezra, either. But, then, I ain't all that sure.

Anyway, there was Tom, and there was Ezra and Jinx—face to face, as it were, like with Miss Claiborne a few months before.

Now, like I said, Tom weren't no midget, as far as turkeys go. And Jinx—he was pretty good size hisself.

Even from where I was, a good fifty yards away, I swear I saw the hackles rise on the back of old Jinx's neck, as he strained against the rope holding him to Ezra's wagon. At the same time I saw Tom's tail feathers begin to quiver. There was a glint in Ezra's eyes and a wicked grin spread across his God-ugly face.

Without taking his eyes off of Tom, Ezra reached down and, with a swift flick of the big bowie knife he always carried, cut the rope holding Jinx.

The dog lunged forward and was all over Tom like a thirsty man on a glass of cold beer. At least, that's the way it appeared at first. But before anyone could tell, Tom jumped up in the air and raked one of his spurs down across Jinx's head, splitting that sucker wide open from just between the ears clear to the dog's upper lip, including right down the middle of his nose. I couldn't have done a neater job with one of the big carving knives I use.

I tell you, sir, that stopped old Jinx dead in his tracks, and he let out a yelp that you could'a heard over in Crownsville. Blood came a pouring off his head like that little waterfall at the head of Lawson's Creek. And when Tom jumped up in the air a second time preparing to give Jinx another go 'round, that dog turned tail and bolted out of town faster'n you could say "skedaddle."

Ezra, he got the meanest look on his face, all scowled up, and I saw him pick up his shotgun. There weren't no question in my mind what he meant to do.

But before he could get the gun to his shoulder Sheriff Pomeroy was standing by the wagon, pistol drawn and pointed at Ezra's chest.

"I reckon you ought to think twice about what you was plannin' to do," said the sheriff.

By this time, two or three other fellows had gathered around the wagon, each one brandishing a gun.

Ezra laid the gun back in the wagon bed real slow like, picked up the reins, and backed the horses down the street until he could turn the wagon around. Then he lit out almost as fast as Jinx had minutes before.

When we all looked to where Tom had been standing, we

saw him marching down the street, still on his way to the back of the feed and grain store. Guess he wasn't about to let anything stop him from having lunch.

From that day on, Tom ruled the roost, so to speak.

\*\*\*\*\*

In the spring of the following year, me and Wilford Lewis was sitting out on the porch in front of my shop early one morning. The air was cool, and it was so quiet we could hear the sun coming up over Gray Mountain. Then, from the silence, came a noise that sounded like someone drumming. Since there hadn't been any Indians in these parts for quite a spell, we knew it weren't them.

"What is that?" asked Wilford, screwing up his face in bewilderment.

"Beats me," I said.

We got up and headed in the direction from where the drumming was coming. As we got closer, Wilford beckoned for me to be careful, to not make a sound. Coming up over a little rise, we were startled to see Old Tom strutting and gobbling like crazy, while six or seven hen turkeys looked on with some interest.

"Son of a gun!" whispered Wilford. "He's a lookin' for a mate!"

"Come on," I whispered back. "Let's get out of here and leave him do his courting in peace."

For the next month or so, there was no sign of Tom in town. Everyone knew what was up, as Wilford was quick to spread the word of what we'd seen.

As spring wore on, the gobbling became less and less, until at last it stopped altogether. We all knew what that meant: Old Tom had met with success. And more than once, too, as toms are wont to do—especially a tom as magnificent as Tom.

By early summer Tom had resumed his daily forays into Camptown. None of the hens or poults ever accompanied him, although they could be seen in great abundance right outside of town.

*****

It was about six years after Tom first showed up in Camptown when it happened.

By this time, Mrs. Buhlig's baby had grown into a little boy, and he'd been followed by a baby sister, whom Tom took a liking to, same as he had her brother some years earlier.

The sun had just gone down and a dusty haze was settling over the town when Tom showed up for his dinner. All of a sudden we heard a bloodcurdling scream coming from the direction of the general store. I looked up to see Mrs. Buhlig wielding her parasol, trying her best to beat off what at first I thought was a large dog. But when I looked closer, I realized what it was: a cougar! And the animal had little Katrina between its jaws, trying to drag the baby away!

I jumped to my feet and ran toward the store. But before I could get there a whirlwind of feathers and spurs descended on the cougar, beating and clawing at it.

For a moment the big animal was caught off guard by its attacker, and in that split second opened its mouth to defend itself, which allowed the baby to drop to the ground.

Mrs. Buhlig snatched the child up and ran for the store.

By now it was apparent to me and to the other bystanders what had laid into the cougar—it was Tom! And although he was clearly no match for an animal four times his weight, he put up a good fight for about two or three minutes—long enough to allow Sheriff Pomeroy to get an open shot at the

66

cougar, killing it.

Tom lay on the ground, blood from the numerous claw and tooth marks the cougar managed to inflict coating his magnificent plumage. There was no doubt in anyone's mind the wounds were fatal.

Every woman and child gathered there was awash in tears, and more than one man—myself included—was crying right along with them.

Tom was given a proper funeral and burial, as befits a hero, and six months later a life-size statue of him, cast in bronze by some sculptor guy in Louisville and paid for by the townsfolk, was erected in front of the feed and grain store.

You can still see it there to this day.

## WOOLLY WANDA
### 1919 – 1928

For my twelfth birthday, my pap took me to the carnival over in Crownsville. He'd told my mom we were going to the Tipsy Toad Saloon so he could teach me how to play pool. My mom didn't much fancy the Tipsy Toad. She thought it was a place where the men went to drink and swap tall tales—which was true. But in her mind a saloon was a far sight better place to go than any carnival, which she considered to be downright sinful, being as how they had all those hootchy-kootchy dancers, not to mention the grifters and their shell games.

The year was 1919, and the nation was getting back to normal after the war.

For my pap, two exciting events happened that year. The first came on July 4th, when Pap took the train to Toledo, Ohio, with three of his buddies to watch Jack Dempsey take on Jess Willard in a boxing match for the heavyweight championship of the world. Ever since Pap whipped John L. Sullivan in a wrestling match when he was a teenager, he'd been a big fan of the sport of pugilism—professional pugilism, that is.

The second was when Pap's beloved Cincinnati Reds defeated the Chicago White Sox in the World Series. Of course, the following year it came out the Sox threw the series, a fact my pap never fully accepted since he knew the Reds were, without a doubt, the better team, and didn't have to have the championship handed to them.

My mom held an entirely different view of what was important. For her, the most significant event of 1919 was Congress approving the 19th Amendment to the Constitution, giving women—including her—the right to vote.

Overshadowing all of this was something that was about to happen that would change the face of America forever. In January, the 18th Amendment had been ratified, and on January 16th of the following year, the nation went dry. Prohibition had become the law of the land.

I tell all this to put into perspective that what seemed important to adults—like my pap and my mom—was not the stuff that was important to a twelve-year-old kid, namely, me, because the most important thing that happened to me in 1919 happened that night at the carnival, on my birthday.

That's when I met Woolly Wanda.

The first thing Pap and I did when we arrived at the carnival was to search out Candy Stearman. Pap knew Candy would have brought along his moonshine to sell, and Pap dearly loved Candy's moonshine. It took a few minutes to find him, and Pap settled in to throw back a couple of pints. Handing me a fifty-cent piece, he told me to go have some fun—and stay out of trouble.

For the next half hour, I wandered around the grounds. Mom was right about the grifters—one of them took me for a nickle. I *swear* I knowed which shell that pea was under!

I ended up, finally, at the freak show.

Now, I lived in Camptown, Kentucky. And this was the first carnival I'd ever been to, so I wasn't used to seeing what freaks looked like. And at that time, I didn't even know *I* was one.

I watched while the rubber man twisted himself into such a pretzel I knew for sure he wouldn't be able to get out. But he did. Next came the sword swallower. I almost puked watching him shove a sword down his throat.

And then she came out.

I'd seen her name on the canvas that covered the front of the tent behind the stage: *Woolly Wanda*. But there was no picture of her, and I sure didn't know what Woolly Wanda did. It turned out, it wasn't what she *did*, it was what she *was*.

A veil covered her face, so I couldn't see it. But her arms and lower legs were showing. I stared at them: they were covered with hair—even more than mine, and I had a lot of hair for a twelve-year-old. *That's no woman*, was the first thought that popped into my head. *That's a man*.

The barker began his spiel.

"Ladies and gents come right in and see Woolly Wanda, the bearded girl. You think this is a lot of hair?" He pointed with his cane to Wanda's legs. "You ain't seen nothing yet! Wait 'til you see her face! Come on, gents—one thin dime; a mere ten cents for the thrill of a lifetime!"

The barker went on to describe the other incredible acts we'd see inside if we paid our dime, but I didn't hear what they were. I couldn't take my eyes off of Wanda. She wasn't a woman, she was a girl, the barker said. *How old?* I wondered.

When Wanda ducked back behind the canvas, joining the Rubber Man and the sword swallower, I got in line with the rest of the people, mostly men, plus a couple of boys, and a woman or two.

Inside, it took a few minutes for my eyes to get accustomed to the dim light provided by the kerosene lamps. Along with the crowd, I moved through passageways formed by canvas on either side. A few feet and we came to a small stage about a foot off the ground where the Rubber Man performed more

70

unbelievable contortions than he had outside. In the next area on another stage was the flame thrower. After him was the sword swallower, followed by the fat lady. I began to despair we might not get to see Wanda.

And then . . . there she was.

I'd rounded a corner of the passageway, having left the rest of the crowd behind, and saw her sitting on a chair on a small stage no more than six feet from me, her body swathed in light from several lamps placed nearby.

The barker was right: she had a full beard. Not too long, because she was only a girl, but a full beard nonetheless. Again, I stared, amazed at the sight before me.

I looked up from the beard and saw her eyes.

And I fell in love!

They were the most beautiful eyes I had ever seen. Even in the dim light, I saw they were a pale green, large and expressive—and sad. She looked so sad. My heart began to ache.

I smiled. Slowly, a smile crossed her face, a face framed by long flowing black hair that matched the color of her beard, as black as the inside of the cave on old man Prockett's farm. Under that growth of hair, I knew it was a beautiful face, a face beautiful enough to match her eyes.

"Hi," I whispered. It was still just her and me in this little stage area.

"Hi," she whispered back.

"My name's Marcus," I whispered again.

"I'm Wanda," she said.

"I know."

Right then four or five men and some boys came around the corner. When they saw Wanda they began to laugh, pointing at her.

"Freak, freak!" shouted one of the boys.

"Damn, Benny, she's got more hair on her face than you do," one man said to his friend.

"I wonder if she's got hair all over her body," said another man. "Hey, honey, how about taking your clothes off so's we can see if you got hair all over your body."

I felt so embarrassed—for myself; for Wanda? I wasn't sure—that I hurried on through the rest of the passageways, not stopping to see the midget or the man who was supposed to be seven feet tall.

Once outside the tent, I made my way to a stand where a man sold ice cream cones. I'd never had ice cream in a cone, so I bought one and headed out to find my pap. When I got to where I'd left him, Candy said he'd left a few minutes before, heading for the girlie show.

I figured it would be a while before Pap came back, so I wandered back through the carnival grounds.

I'm not sure how I found myself behind the freak show tent, but there I was. I'd bought another ice cream cone and was sitting on a pickle keg eating it when I saw her slip out. Although it was dark, I knew it was Wanda.

"Wanda," I said in a low voice.

She stopped and squinted to see where the words came from. "Who's there?" she asked, a hint of concern in her voice.

"It's Marcus."

"From inside, a little while ago?"

"Yes."

She walked over to where I sat. "What are you eating?" she asked.

"An ice cream cone."

"I've never had an ice cream cone. My daddy says it'd get all over my beard."

"Is that a real beard?" I asked.

Wanda nodded.

"Have you had it all your life?"

"I've been hairy all my life. The beard started about a year ago."

"You want a lick of my ice cream?" I asked.

For a moment, Wanda hesitated.

"Okay," she said finally.

I held out the cone to her. She took it and licked it.

"Ooh, this is good," she said, "and cold."

"How old are you?" I asked.

"Twelve. How old are you?"

"I'm twelve, too. Today's my birthday."

"Happy birthday. What happened to your arm?"

I looked down at my left arm. It was withered, about a third as long as my right arm. I was the last of six children, the first five being girls. My pap always wanted a boy. He dreamed of his son becoming either a champion boxer or playing with the Reds. With my arm, neither of those dreams became realities.

"I was born that way," I said.

"Like I was born hairy," said Wanda.

"I guess that makes us both freaks, doesn't it?" I said.

We laughed.

I heard my pap's voice calling me.

"I have to go," I said. "It was nice meeting you. You've got beautiful eyes." And I was off and running before she could say anything.

*****

Six years passed before I saw Wanda again when the carnival returned to Crownsville.

By this time both my mom and Pap had passed away. I was eighteen, and working the farm with two of my sisters and their husbands. One other sister had died, and the other two

73

moved away, one to Louisville, the other to Cynthiana.

When I heard the carnival was coming back I wondered if Wanda was still with it. I'd never forgotten her in all that time.

I drove over to Crownsville, parked the truck, and made a beeline for the freak show tent. When I saw her name, this time with her picture, on the front of the tent canvas, my heart skipped a beat. Now she was billed as the Bearded "Lady." Unlike six years earlier, she was not one of the acts that enticed the crowd to come in.

I paid my twenty cents and went in. Bypassing the acts at the front of the passageway, I hurried along until I saw her sitting there on her chair.

She was more beautiful than I remembered.

The beard was longer, as was her hair. And she'd developed breasts.

She looked up when she saw me and smiled. And those eyes!

"Hi, Marcus," she said.

My mouth fell open. "You remembered?"

"My first ice cream cone? How could I forget?"

I laughed. "How about meeting me behind the tent later, and I'll buy you another?"

"Okay."

Spectators began to catch up to me. I turned and left.

About an hour later, I spotted her coming out of the back of the tent.

"Where's my ice cream cone?" she asked, her eyes sparkling.

"I didn't want it to melt. Wait here, and I'll be right back."

I wasn't gone more than two or three minutes, but when I reached the corner of the tent I heard muffled sounds coming from where I'd left Wanda. Rounding the tent, I saw see three men holding her down on the ground.

"Come on, babe," said one of the men. "We're going to take your shirt off to see if you got hairy tits."

Dropping the cone, I charged toward the trio like a crazed bull. The one bending over Wanda had his back to me, and when I reached him I gave him a hard kick right in his testicles. He dropped like a rock. The other two men spun around to face me, and I smashed my fist into one's mouth, which sent him reeling back against a tree. The third man hesitated for a second, then took off running. Apparently, his desire to know if Wanda's breasts were hairy was not as great as not wanting to get a beating.

I helped Wanda up from the ground and we quickly retreated to the safety of the tent.

"Are you all right?" I asked when we were back inside.

She nodded, still too shaken to speak. She looked up at me, her eyes thankful, and at the same time questioning.

I answered her question by gently placing my lips on hers. Even through the hair, they felt sweet and soft and moist.

"I've never kissed anyone before," she said when I pulled back.

"I've never kissed anyone with a beard before," I said.

We both started laughing so hard we were crying.

"How long are you in town?" I asked.

"Three more days."

"I'll be by every day."

Three days later the carnival left town. Wanda and I started corresponding, she writing me about all the places where the carnival was playing, I in turn telling her about the farm.

In June of 1928, the carnival was in a little town outside of Nashville, Tennessee. Without telling Wanda, I drove down to surprise her. It would be a double surprise because by now I had also grown a beard.

When I walked down the passageway and stopped before

her, she looked up, for a moment not recognizing me. Then her eyes lit up, and she jumped up off the chair, embraced me, and kissed me. By this time other spectators had caught up to me. Looking past Wanda, I saw the astonishment on their faces.

"Come on," I said, taking her hand and pulling her after me.

Outside I took her in my arms again and kissed her.

"Marry me," I whispered.

"What?"

"Marry me. I love you."

She pulled back from me. "I'm a freak. You can't love me."

I held up my left arm. "Takes one to know one. I love you. Marry me."

Two weeks later we were married back in Camptown.

Wanda told me she didn't like my beard, so I shaved it off in time for the wedding. To my amazement, she'd shaved hers off, too. In fact, she'd shaved her whole body. I had to admit: she was more beautiful without the hair.

As part of our wedding vows, I promised to keep my beard off, to shave every day.

Wanda promised the same. But only the beard, she said.

I'd just have to learn to live with her hairy arms and legs.

## MY GRANDFATHER'S GRANDFATHER CLOCK
## 1922

*Tick, Tock, Tick, Tock, Tick, Tock.*

I stood in the hallway staring at the clock. It was a grandfather clock; my Grandfather Townsend's clock. Did that make it my grandfather's grandfather clock? I wondered.

From the time I was a little boy, no more than two or three years old, I would stand in front of the clock, my head tipped back, trying to see all the way to the top, where a carved wooden eagle made its home. I knew the clock was tall, much taller than anyone in my family—then, again, everyone in my family was kind of short anyway. But it wasn't until I was eleven I discovered just how tall it was.

One day my cousin, Danny, and I got a tape measure from my grandma's sewing basket, and a chair from the kitchen. While I teetered on the chair and held the end of the tape measure up to the tip of the eagle's beak—his head was thrust upward, toward the ceiling, which made his beak the tallest point on the clock—Danny pulled the tape taut, to see what it measured where it met the floor: eight feet, three inches. Just then Grandpa came down the stairs.

"What are you boys up to?" he asked.

"We wanted to see how tall the clock was, Grandpa," I said. "That's all."

"Did you find out?"

"Yes, sir," said Danny, "It's—"

"Eight feet, three inches," interrupted Grandpa.

Danny's jaw dropped. "How'd you know that?"

"Same way as you fellers. I measured it once. About the time I was your age. Ain't got any shorter or taller since then, has it?"

"Nope. Still the same;" said Danny, "eight feet, three inches."

"Exactly half again as tall as me," said Grandpa.

"Really?" I said. "So, how tall does that make you, Grandpa?"

"Can't you figure it out?" he asked.

"Maybe. But you could just tell us," I said.

Grandpa grinned. "Exactly five feet, six inches."

As I climbed down off the chair I was struck by the fact my grandpa wasn't much taller than either Danny or me—and we were only eleven.

"You reckon either of us will ever be as tall as your clock?" I asked, one of those stupid questions eleven-year-old boys are prone to throw out there from time to time.

Grandpa laughed. "Not likely. But, for sure, you'll be taller than I am. Now, come on. I think your grandma's taken a mincemeat pie from the oven, and she'll need someone who's not biased to tell her whether it's any good or not."

*****

Grandpa was right. Neither Danny nor I ever grew to be anywhere close to eight feet tall.

But we both did come close to six feet which, for our family, almost qualified us as giants.

Now, here I was, once again standing in front of the clock.

I didn't have to tilt my head back so far to see the eagle like when I was younger. And it was much easier to appreciate the rest of the clock, too, since I was taller and it still had not grown any.

Grandpa told me all about the clock once, how it was built by a local watchmaker here in Camptown whose single attempt at a timepiece of this magnitude was this particular instrument. Otherwise, his work was restricted to pocket watches and mantle clocks. My grandfather's clock was definitely too large for a mantle!

The wood was solid mahogany, and mahogany veneer, and with all the working "innards" it contained, weighed—according to Grandpa—almost exactly the same as he did, even though—as we had learned as children—it was exactly half again as tall as he was. The numbers on the face were Roman Numerals; no wonder it took me so long to figure out how to tell time with this clock! The upper half of the face contained a beautiful, wooded scene painted on it: two deer placidly drinking from a pond surrounded by trees and a soaring, snow-capped, mountain in the background. A montage of carved animals—bears, raccoons, wolves, what have you—marched in a parade around the top, which was crowned by that imposing eagle that reigned over the whole assemblage. Spiraled, wooden columns descended elegantly down all four sides, ending at four huge claw feet that supported the whole structure.

The bottom part of the case consisted of three glass sides, and a solid wooden back. Inside, hung a magnificent brass pendulum, and three weight-driven chimes. It was an "eight-day" clock, but Grandpa reset the counterweights every seven days.

"Just to play it safe," he would say.

The way Grandpa told it, his daddy, my great-grandpa,

bought the clock the day Grandpa was born.

"Papa'd been eyeing that clock in old man Morse's store for a few months before I was born," Grandpa said. "He fell in love with that clock. But it was too expensive, much more than Papa could afford, with a baby on the way. He wanted his first child—that'd be me—to be a boy. 'I don't care if the next six are girls,' he'd told Momma, 'so long as the first one's a boy.'

"So when I was born," Grandpa continued, "and Papa discovered he had a son, he drove his wagon right down to Mr. Morse's store. It was so early the store hadn't opened yet. But Papa wasn't about to wait. He banged on the door until he got Mr. Morse out of bed—he lived in an apartment right above the shop, you see—and made him come down and sell Papa the clock. When Papa got it home and Momma found out what he'd done, she was furious. She would have killed him if she wasn't still bedfast from having me.

"'Why'd you buy that thing?' she cried. 'You know we can't afford it.'

"'Annabel, I just had a son,' my pa answered her. 'The clock's for him. I made a deal with old man Morse. I'll do some extra work for him to pay for it.' And that clock's been standing right there in this hallway ever since."

"What about the plaque?" I'd asked. There was a brass plaque at the clock's base, attached to it by four screws. The plaque read:

*property of*
*Wilbur Eugene Townsend*
*born November 11th, 1832*

Grandpa chuckled. "That was your great-grandma's doing. She told Papa if this really was *my* clock, she wanted my name on it. That way, if times got tough for them—and they did— they could never sell the clock because it belonged to me."

80

\*\*\*\*\*

Ninety years. The clock had stood in this same spot for ninety years, from the day Grandpa was born in this very house. Now he lay dying; upstairs, in the same room in which he had come into this world.

We'd known for almost a year about the cancer. At first, the doctors thought they'd gotten it all when they operated. But it came back. Two months ago, Grandpa started to go downhill, fast. Now, it was only a matter of time, hours, actually, the doctor said. All the family—all who still lived in and around Camptown—had come back home to say their final good-byes to the old man.

I heard the front door open. It had been opening a lot today, with people coming and going. Then I heard a familiar voice.

"Hey, Buck, how you doing?"

I turned to see Danny standing in the doorway. It had been more than ten years since I'd last seen him, ever since Uncle Andy packed his family up and moved them off to Florida. Danny and I were both sixteen at the time. Grandma and Grandpa had been devastated. Aunt Lucille was the first of their children to move away from home. I'd been devastated too: Danny was my closest friend.

We'd kept in touch over the years, by letters and cards. But somehow, every time Danny made it back home I was either away at college or serving in the army, fighting in Europe.

"Hey, Danny," I said. We hugged each other, holding tight for a long time. "I'm fine. How are you?"

"Good," he replied.

He stepped back to look at me.

"God, you're getting old," he said.

We both laughed.

"How's Grandpa?" he asked.

"Not good. It's just a matter of time."

"That's what I heard. Who's up there with him now?"

"Grandma and the doctor."

"You think I might go up?"

"Give it a minute. Grandma asked everyone to wait down here for a bit, while the doctor does whatever it is he's doing."

Danny looked at the clock. "Still here. Hey, you remember the time we measured this sucker to see how tall it was?"

I smiled. "I was just thinking about that when you came in."

Neither of us said anything for a few minutes. The only sound was that of the clock measuring time.

*Tick, Tock, Tick, Tock, Tick, To. . .*

Suddenly the silence in the hallway was deafening.

"What happened?" asked Danny.

"The clock stopped," I said.

"The clock never stops. Grandpa must have forgot to set the weights."

"I set the weights yesterday," I said. "I've been coming over Sundays before church for the last month to set them, ever since Grandpa became bedfast."

I looked at the hands. They had stopped at four minutes after five.

By this time several people had emptied out into the hallway from the parlor.

"What happened?" my Uncle Edgar asked.

"The clock stopped," said Danny.

We all stood and stared at the clock as if by our collective wills we could make it start up again.

"He's gone."

We looked up to see Grandma at the top of the stairs.

"He's gone," she said again. "He passed a few minutes

82

ago."

I looked back at the clock. "I'll be damned," I murmured.

*****

The next day I stopped by to see how Grandma was getting along. They'd taken Grandpa's body to Jacobson's Funeral Home the night before. The service was scheduled for Thursday. When I walked into the house, I knew at once something was different; there was no sound coming from my grandfather's grandfather clock.

I found Grandma in the kitchen, staring out the window, sipping her morning cup of coffee.

"They couldn't fix it," she said before I had a chance to say anything.

"Couldn't fix what?" I asked. But, I knew what she was talking about.

"The clock. I had Mr. Van Pelt come over first thing this morning to see about fixing the clock. He looked it over real good, then told me he couldn't fix it. He said all the parts were so worn out it was a wonder the thing lasted this long. Said by the time he got through replacing all the parts, it'd be a completely different clock. I told him never mind."

"You okay?" I asked.

She nodded. "I'll be fine."

"You're having the service here at the house?"

"It's what he would have wanted."

*****

The day of the funeral dawned bright and clear, one of those typical, brisk, Kentucky, November days. I was the first one at the house.

When I walked through the front door, I was struck again by the eerie stillness of a hallway that had not known silence for ninety years until Grandpa's death.

Then I saw it: the empty space in the hallway. The clock was gone!

I hurried into the parlor, hoping to find Grandma so I could find out what happened to the clock. She wasn't there, but Grandpa's coffin was. The undertaker had brought it earlier that morning.

It was the first time I had seen the casket. Grandma insisted on going to the funeral home alone and picking it out by herself.

I was surprised at its length. Grandpa was a short man, but the casket looked to be enormous, over eight feet long, I calculated. I walked over and looked in . . . and started laughing, laughing so hard I was crying.

Inside laid Grandpa, much as I remembered him, although considerably thinner. So thin, in fact, he fit nicely inside the clock case which, in turn, rested neatly inside the coffin. There he lay inside the glass cabinet, his arms folded peacefully over his chest. The pendulum and chimes and weights had been removed and lay in the casket on either side of the case.

I looked once more at the painted, wooded scene, the animals on their journey around the top, and that wonderful, imposing, glorious, eagle. The clock hands still pointed to the time of grandpa's death: 5:04.

I lifted the clock's glass door, bent down, and kissed my grandpa on the forehead.

"Goodbye, Grandpa," I said. "You have a good time."

## WHEN THE LEAVES FALL
## 1927 – 1933

It was freezing cold that January morning when Momma got us out of bed, made us get dressed, and packed what few possessions we had. We walked the two miles to the bus depot—Daddy had long since sold the Buick—shivering from the wind whipping through our threadbare coats. We caught the first bus heading south, and the next day found ourselves in Camptown, Kentucky, where Gramps picked us up at the depot in his old farm truck.

Six months later, June 2, 1931, the day after my tenth birthday, we all watched Daddy head down the lane leading from the houses to the road: Grandpa and Grandma Cartee; Grandma's aunt, Eunice; my mother; my four younger brothers; my sister; and me. He'd have a six-mile walk into town, where he planned to hop a train, eventually making his way back to Detroit, the same city he had moved us from some five months earlier.

We children all thought the bus ride to Kentucky a great adventure. My brothers thought Daddy's train ride sounded like even more fun. But I knew Daddy wasn't taking any passenger train. He didn't have any money for that. He'd be riding in boxcars, like so many of the men I'd seen back home before we left.

None of us wanted to see him go. But we knew the little patch of land that passed for Gramps and Grandma's farm was barely enough to provide for them and Great-aunt Eunice, who lived with them, let alone two more adults and six kids. So Daddy decided to head back north, see if he could find some work in Detroit, so he could send us some money.

"If there's nothing there," he said, "I'll head on up north to cherry country, and try to get a job picking cherries, and whatever else I can find after that."

Now he was leaving. We were all crying, all except Gramps, whom I never remember ever seeing cry.

"When will Daddy come back?" I asked my mother, through my tears.

She put one arm around my shoulder. "When the leaves fall, Rosemarie," she said. "When the leaves fall your daddy'll be back."

I looked at the big maple tree that stood in Gramp's front yard, its branches bursting with leaves. That would be my calendar, I reckoned. When all the leaves were gone from the maple, Daddy would be back.

As we watched him disappear into the distance, I thought about how we came to be here, and what had transpired over the last several years.

It wasn't always like this.

\*\*\*\*\*

We'd lived in a little house on Forrester Street we rented from Mr. Peabody. We moved there in 1927 when Patrick and Michael were born. Having twins, on top of Angela and my two younger brothers and me, forced Momma and Daddy to move out of the small bungalow they'd rented when they first got married.

Our new home was an old, two-story, white-frame house, hardly big enough for a family of eight. The downstairs consisted of a parlor, dining room, and kitchen. Upstairs were three bedrooms, one for Momma and Daddy and the new twins, one for the two older boys, and one for Angela and me. An outhouse next to the shed made for some chilly walks on cold winter days—and nights!

We had a coal furnace, but the ducts only ran to the downstairs. The second floor was warmed by whatever heat managed to find its way up through the single register in the floor of each bedroom. The registers also served as a means for Angela and me to hear whatever conversation went on in the kitchen directly below our bedroom, and the place where Momma and Daddy always held their "serious" conversations.

There were happy times on Forrester Street. There were lots of other kids in the neighborhood to play with, and the school was about a mile-and-a-half away, which made it easy to walk to. I started first grade the fall after we moved in.

Since my brothers and sisters weren't old enough to be in school yet, Momma stayed home to watch them, while Daddy went to work at the Fisher Body Plant that had opened not too long before.

Almost every Sunday—the one day Daddy was off from work—we'd all pile into the Buick after church and head out to Belle Isle Park for a picnic.

What I remember best though, is those Sundays when the Tigers were in town. Daddy and I—just the two of us—we'd go out to old Navin Field to watch them play. I was the only one of Daddy's children to ever share his love of baseball. Our favorite player was Dale Alexander—everybody called him "Moose"—who played first base. The Tigers had a terrible team in 1929, but "Moose" was terrific: he hit .343 with 25 home runs and 137 runs batted in.

Saturday nights, Daddy hauled the big washtub from the back porch into the kitchen, and Momma filled it with hot water she heated in big pots on the stove.

One by one, each of us kids would get our bath, followed by a big tablespoon of castor oil, washed down with a glass of Coca-Cola and popcorn to go along with our Cokes. Being the oldest, I took my bath first. I'm sure by the time the two older boys got their turn—Momma always washed the babies in the sink—the water wasn't only cool—if not downright cold—but hardly clean enough to do the job.

Unfortunately, those good times were about to come to an end.

*****

We were all excited with Halloween around the corner in two days. The year was 1929. I was eight years old and in third grade.

I thought Daddy was acting strange when he came home from work that night. He was real quiet, which was unusual for him.

Right after we finished eating, Momma made us all go to bed, which was also unusual, since we normally got to stay up for at least an hour after supper.

It was a chilly night, so while Angela jumped straight into the double bed she and I shared, I slipped over to the register and straddled it, letting the warm air swirl up under my nightgown. I heard Momma and Daddy talking.

"You heard what happened today?" asked Daddy.

"Yes," answered Momma. "What's it mean?"

"Means there's going to be rough times ahead. A lot of people lost their life savings today. They ain't going to be in any hurry to go out and buy a new car anytime soon. I might

88

lose my job."

I heard Momma start to cry.

"Hell, I ain't lost it yet," said Daddy, gruffly. "So there ain't no reason to go all blubbery."

"What will we do if you do?" asked Momma, still crying.

"We'll cross that bridge when we come to it," said Daddy.

*****

That first winter wasn't too bad. Daddy took a cut in pay, but fortunately, we'd already put in a load of coal. We knew we'd keep warm through the cold months. Then, right before Christmas, his workweek was cut from six days to five—no more Saturdays. Three weeks later Daddy's hours were cut back again, this time from five days to three. Mr. Livingston, who owned the little grocery store at the end of our street, was kind enough to give Momma a line of credit.

The final blow came in April when Daddy got laid off completely—the same day Mr. Livingston said he'd have to start getting paid in cash since we now owed him more than one hundred and fifty dollars.

After three weeks of standing in the unemployment line and looking, without success, for another job, Daddy reluctantly agreed to let Momma take in ironing to help out with the bills. He did manage to pick up an odd job here and there, and for a while received two dollars and ninety-five cents a week from the city relief fund, but that lasted only a short time. Meanwhile, we were getting further and further behind on our rent.

Summer came and passed.

There were no more trips to Belle Isle Park. No more baseball games.

*****

One day I noticed Momma wasn't wearing her wedding ring.

"Did you lose it?" I asked.

Momma's lower lip quivered. "No, honey," she said. "Daddy and I pawned our rings, so we could buy some food and pay a few bills. But soon as everything gets back to normal, we'll go get them out."

*****

"I'm going to do it."

I heard Daddy's voice coming up through the register, followed by Momma's.

"I can't bear the thought of you having to do that." She was crying.

"Dammit woman, if I can't *sell* any apples, at least we can eat them!" Then, in a low voice, he added, "Sometimes I wish to hell we wasn't Catholic."

"Why would you say that?" asked Momma.

"Then we wouldn't have so many mouths to feed."

I was lying on the floor to better hear what was being said, and from my vantage point, I saw the top of Daddy's head where he sat at the kitchen table.

The next thing I knew Momma got up, walked around the table, and slapped Daddy across the face.

"Don't you *ever* say anything like that again!" shouted my mother.

Daddy began to cry. "I'm sorry," he said. "I didn't mean it. It's just . . . it's just . . ."

"I know," said Momma, cradling his head in her arms. "I know."

The next day Momma told us Daddy had a new job, selling apples on a street corner. It was temporary, she hastened to add, until a real job came along.

But a real job never did come along.

Food got scarcer and scarcer. Our clothes became so worn we couldn't go to school any longer, as we'd freeze to death getting there. Our electricity was shut off and the only fuel we had for the furnace was what we found along the railroad tracks that ran behind our house: coal that fell off the coal cars that passed by on a daily basis. That, and the sticks and branches we managed to scavenge from the little stand of trees on the other side of the tracks. Even at that, the house was heated barely above freezing, and most nights we all slept in the parlor, on the floor, as the upstairs was unbearably cold.

The day came when Mr. Peabody showed up on our front step. I heard him tell Momma he couldn't carry us any longer; we'd have to move.

The next day we left for Kentucky.

*****

Thanksgiving, 1931.

It had been almost six months since Daddy had gone back to Detroit. He hadn't found any work there, so he'd headed on up to Traverse City, where he found a job picking cherries. After the harvest ended, he'd gotten another job on a fishing boat.

Twice a month, we'd get a letter and a money order from him. One time he wrote he wished he could write every week, but with postage being two cents, he couldn't afford it.

I continued to keep an eye on the maple tree. Slowly, but surely, the leaves began to fall until, a few days before Christmas, a single one remained, clinging stubbornly to its branch way up at the top of the tree.

By January first it was still there.

The end of January came and went, and still that one leaf refused to fall. I got to where I hated that leaf. If it hadn't been so far up in the tree, and if I wasn't so afraid of heights, I would have climbed up there and ripped it down myself.

Spring came, and with it, the tree started to regain its foliage. By March it was covered with leaves. I knew now Daddy wouldn't be home anytime soon.

We continued to receive letters and checks from him every other week until June, when he wrote that, because of the postage increase to three cents, he'd have to cut back to once a month. This greatly saddened all of us.

Summer passed into autumn, and autumn into winter. Once again the maple began to lose its leaves until, by the middle of December, one leaf again dangled from its branches. And I swear it was the same doggone leaf that was there last year!

The week before Christmas, Angela and I were out playing in the front yard when it happened. I felt something graze my ear, and when I looked down there was a leaf lying on the ground at my feet. I looked up and saw the old maple tree was completely—and I mean *completely*—naked! Not a single leaf remained on it!

I'd just reached the top of the porch steps in my haste to tell Momma the good news when she came bursting out the front door.

"Daddy's coming home!" she cried. "He's coming home!" She waved the letter in her hand, looking for all the world like she was trying to flag down a cab. Tears streamed down her cheeks.

Sure enough, two days later, we all met Daddy at the bus depot in town. He'd managed to find a job at a small machine shop, and on January 7—two years to the day since we'd left Detroit—we moved back home.

*****

What was it that caused me to remember all of this, events that happened some sixty years ago?

Oh, yes—the question my great-grandson, Timmy, asked me as he and my granddaughter, Elsie, were leaving the room I now call home at the Longacre Nursing Center.

"Great-grandma Rosie," he'd said, "when will *you* be coming home?"

You see, I'd lived with Elsie and her family the last four years before my condition got so bad three months ago I entered a care facility.

I looked at Timmy, a bright five-year-old, who'd brought me books in the morning for me to read to him, and tea and cookies in the afternoon for little parties, just the two of us. He couldn't remember when I hadn't been a part of his life.

"When will I be coming home?" I repeated his question. "Why, Timmy, when the leaves fall, that's when I'll go home."

He glanced out at the big oak tree outside my window.

"They're all gone now," he said.

I looked out.

"No," I said, "you see the one desperately hanging on up there, about halfway up?"

"Oh, yes," he said.

"When that one falls, that's when I'll be going home."

"Okay, we'll see you soon, Nana."

Then they were gone.

I put my hand to my chest and took the ring that hung from a chain around my neck between my fingers: my mother's wedding ring she bequeathed me.

I looked out the window again. The wind had picked up, and I saw the branches of the tree start to bend and sway in rhythm with it.

And then the leaf fell.

I watched it drift down, battling the little currents that seemed intent on keeping it airborne until it landed on the sill outside my window.

I sighed and lay my head back on the pillow.

The leaves had fallen. It was time for me to go home. And I was ready.

## THE MALE POOCH BARN
## 1930

My father looked at the field spread out before us, spat a gigantic wad of tobacco juice onto the ground at his feet, and proceeded to wipe the sleeve of his shirt across his mouth to remove what hadn't completely cleared the large handlebar mustache he sported.

"It's going to be a good year for tobacco, Junior," he said, staring straight ahead. "We'll do all right."

"Yes, sir," I said.

I always agreed with my pa, whether I thought he was right or not. In this particular case, I was pretty sure he wasn't.

The year was 1930. I was twenty-one years old. Five months earlier the Great Depression, as it came to be known, virtually wiped out not only the stock market but the whole economy of the United States; tobacco was no exception. The market just wasn't there anymore. Even if we should have a good crop, there was precious little chance of finding anyone to buy it.

"Maybe we should consider something different this year," I offered, cautiously. "Maybe we should plant corn, or potatoes, or some other vegetable."

I say "cautiously" because my father was not one to readily accept either change or advice. But I felt I needed to put the idea out there. Already, our family, which consisted of Pa and Ma, and my seven younger brothers and sisters and me, had begun to feel the effects of a scarcity of food, due to a lack of income.

Pa looked at me as though I had suggested we leave the Baptist church and become Catholics.

"Boy," he said. He always called me 'boy' when he became irritated with me. "I been growing tobacco on this land since 'fore you was born. I ain't about to change now. Men been chewing tobacco since God made Adam, and they're going to continue to chew, depression or no depression."

Pa liked to back up his beliefs with what he perceived to be facts from the Bible, whether they were or not.

I didn't bother to tell Pa that planting the same crop—namely tobacco—in the same fields year after year instead of rotating them, was one reason we were seeing poorer and poorer harvests every year. Nor did I push the matter any further of possibly making an exception this one year, and planting something else. Once Pa made up his mind, not even God could change it.

And so we went about getting ready for planting. The plant beds were prepared and the seedlings inserted. We plowed the fields—again, and again, and again—and in May we transferred the by-then foot-high plants from the beds into the fields.

Then came the drought.

For over five months barely any rain fell in Chickapea County. Our method was to irrigate the fields with water from the Chickapea River, but it was so low our efforts were useless. Helpless, we watched our plants wither and die in the fields. It wouldn't make any difference if there was a market for tobacco in the fall or not. We wouldn't have any to sell.

It was about then Mr. Everingham showed up.

We weren't used to seeing his kind in our part of Kentucky.

Dressed in a Tweed jacket, wearing knickerbockers, and with a Fedora hat perched cockily to one side of his head, he looked exactly like we would have imagined an English gentleman to look—except he was from Canada as it turned out.

Ma and Pa and I were sitting on the front porch, commiserating about the disaster that had befallen our crops. Rachel and Tom, my teen-aged sister and brother, were inside, and the five younger children were playing in the yard, when an automobile appeared at the end of our lane, kicking up dust as it headed toward the house.

When it drew closer, we saw it was one of those new Oldsmobiles, the kind we'd seen drawings of in advertisements in our local newspaper, but never in person.

The other children—the five in the yard plus Rachel and Tom—joined Ma and Pa and me on the porch. When the car came to a stop everything was so still we could have heard Mrs. Jensen hollering at her husband from their farm a mile away from ours—which we frequently did on some nights when he got in later than she thought he should after a bout of drinking at the Tipsy Toad.

And when Mr. Everingham exited his car and walked toward the porch, it was all we could do to keep from bursting out laughing. If it hadn't been for the stern look on Ma's face, I have no doubt we would have—Pa included.

"Mr. Stanton? I'm Chadwick Everingham."

When Mr. Everingham spoke, all of us—and this time I even saw a grin on Ma's face—had to give it our all to control ourselves. His accent was so thick you could, as my grandfather Biddlemire used to say when the occasional Yankee passed through town, 'cut it with a butter knife.'

"Yes," said Pa as best he could without laughing. "I'm Cornelius Stanton."

"Mr. Stanton, delighted to meet you. I'm interested in your

barn, sir."

Ten heads immediately swiveled toward the barn that stood about a hundred yards from the house, out close to the road.

"My barn?" asked Pa, his astonishment apparent. "Why you interested in my barn?"

"I'd like to paint it, sir."

Paint our barn? Why in the world does this dandy want to paint our barn? It had been there longer than I'd been alive, and in my twenty-one years on earth had never been painted—not that the old thing couldn't stand to be. Whatever paint might have covered the wood at one time had long since been worn away by the wind and rain. Now the barn was just a grimy black.

"Yes, well so would I," said Pa. "But that sure ain't going to happen mister, 'cause I ain't got a extra plugged nickel to pay for it."

"Oh, no, sir," said Mr. Everingham. "I'm not expecting you to pay even a copper. I want to paint your barn at no expense to you."

Now, this was getting interesting. What was this fellow up to?

"You see," continued Mr. Everingham, "I represent the Mail Pouch Tobacco Company. We've undertaken a new advertising campaign of painting our signs on barns like yours, all over the country. It's good advertising for us, and you get a complimentary paint job."

Pa raised one eyebrow. "Complimentary? That be the same as free?" he asked, still obviously not convinced.

"Absolutely free," said Mr. Everingham.

"When would this painting take place?" asked Pa.

"Why, tomorrow, if we can come to an agreement today."

"You going to do the painting?" I asked. If there was a job to be had, I was thinking I was the one to have it. A little spare cash would be mighty welcome.

"Oh, my, no," said Mr. Everingham, laughing. "We normally have our own team of men do the job: however, they're all busy right now in other parts around the county. I've contracted with a Mr. McGinnis to do the job."

"Howard McGinnis?" said Pa. "But he ain't got but one leg. How's he going to do the job?"

"Oh, not him," said Mr. Everingham. "His son: Humphrey. He's the one I've contracted with."

At this, all restraint flew out the window. Pa slapped his knee, shook his head, and laughed so hard I thought he'd kill himself. All the kids were rolling around, laughing as hard as Pa. Even Ma threw her head back and bellowed. I followed suit.

When the laughter died down, Mr. Everingham, who appeared shocked by the whole episode, asked, "Did I say something witty?"

"Mr. . . . ?" said Pa.

"Everingham," answered Mr. Everingham, clearly annoyed now. "Chadwick Everingham."

"Mr. Everingham," said Pa, "I don't know how you come to 'contract,' like you say, with Humphrey McGinnis, but I can tell you, you've made a big mistake."

Pa was right. Humphrey McGinnis, two years older than me, was, again as my grandmother used to say, 'dumb as dirt.' One story I'd heard—now, I can't swear if it's true or not— was that when Humphrey's daddy was laid up with some ailment—the one that eventually led to him losing his leg—he told Humphrey to go out and milk the cow for him. Story goes Humphrey went out to the barn all right—and tried to milk the bull! Now, again, I don't know if that's true or not, but I do know for a fact that on the several occasions I saw Humphrey working out in the field next to where the bull was pastured, that old bull never took his eyes off Humphrey, never turned his back on him.

"Why, what's wrong?" asked Mr. Everingham.

"Why, that boy ain't got the sense God gave a flea," said Pa.

Ma nodded in agreement.

"'Sides," added Pa, "I know for a fact he only made it through the third grade. I ain't sure he even knows how to read or write. How in the world did you ever get hooked up with him?"

Mr. Everingham shifted, uncomfortably. "As you know, his father owns the general store. He said the only way he would continue to carry our product was if we hired his son to do the painting. He said he was sure the boy would do a capital job."

"A 'capital' job, huh?" said Pa. "I hope for your sake you're right. So, what is it you're going to paint on my barn?"

"First of all," said Mr. Everingham, "it's something new we're doing with a select few structures. Most barns we paint are painted black with yellow lettering. But on yours, we're painting it red, with yellow lettering. It will say 'Mail Pouch Tobacco, treat yourself to the best.' The words 'Mail Pouch' will be the largest size letters, naturally, with 'Tobacco' somewhat smaller, and the rest smaller still. That will be on the side of the barn facing the road, but of course, we shall paint the entire barn."

"And Humphrey's going to paint all of that?"

"I'm sure he'll do an excellent job," said Mr. Everingham.

"Okay, then," said Pa, reaching out his hand to Mr. Everingham. "We'll look to see *Mr.* McGinnis here tomorrow."

The next morning Humphrey arrived at our house about ten o'clock, driving his daddy's old Ford truck loaded down with cans of paint and brushes. We found out later that, though he'd been by our place probably a hundred times in his life, he'd gotten lost and wandered around searching for our farm for more than an hour.

It took him the better part of the next two weeks to paint the barn red.

Now, I'm no mental genius myself, but if it had been me doing the job, I would have carried the can of paint up the ladder with me, instead of leaving it on the ground and having to come down each time I needed more paint on my brush. As I said, Humphrey wasn't all that smart. But, hey, I wasn't getting paid to supervise.

Pa said he didn't care how long it took to get the job done, seeing as how he wasn't paying for the work anyway. And, we all had to admit, Humphrey was doing a pretty good job.

The day Humphrey showed up to start painting the letters he brought a telegram with him that had arrived at the telegraph office in town the night before. The telephone line hadn't yet reached our place.

When Ma opened the letter and read it, she let out a little gasp.

"What is it, Jewel," asked Pa. "What's wrong."

"It's Aunt Goldie," said Ma, her voice breaking. "She's done up and died!"

Aunt Goldie was Ma's favorite aunt. When Ma's pa, Grandpa Lewis, died when Ma was no more than seven, Ma's mother and her six children, including Ma, moved in to live with Aunt Goldie. She was almost like a mother to my ma.

"Does it say when the funeral is?" asked Pa.

"Day after tomorrow. Come on, we got a lot to get ready before we leave."

There was no question we'd be going to the funeral, which was to be held up in Columbus, Ohio, where Aunt Goldie moved to when she got older, to be with one of her daughters.

When a relative dies, you go pay your respects.

"What about Humphrey?" asked Pa.

"What about him?" asked Ma.

"We can't leave him here to finish painting our barn with no supervision. Lord knows what he'd end up putting on it."

"Ain't our concern," said Ma, "long as he gets the thing painted. 'Sides, he's done all right up to now. And 'sides that, we'll be back in less than a week. Chances are, at the rate he's been moving, by then he'll have just figured out which side of the barn the letters go on."

We all whooped and hollered. But a few minutes later Pa walked down the lane to the barn where Humphrey was getting his supplies out of the truck, and pointed out to him the side next to the road.

By mid-afternoon, we were on our way, and Humphrey had started on the lettering. In fact, the "M" was almost finished, and it didn't look half bad.

\*\*\*\*\*

It was after midnight when we got back home on Friday.

The next morning Ma let us sleep late. We'd hardly set down at the table for breakfast when Pa came rushing in through the kitchen door, his face red from laughing so hard. It took a few minutes before he could get any words out.

"Y'all come see this," he said.

We all threw our jackets on and followed Pa out the door and down the lane to the road. When we reached the end of the lane Pa stopped and whirled around.

"Did you ever?" he said, pointing toward the barn.

We all looked to see what he was pointing at, and then broke out in hysterical laughter, even the little kids who couldn't read.

On the barn, in brilliant yellow letters on a red background, were the words

## MALE POOCH
## TOBACCO

It was a beautiful job of painting, even if the spelling did leave something to be desired!

"*Male Pooch*?" I said, tears rolling down my cheeks. "What the heck is 'Male Pooch'?"

"Durned if I know," said Pa, laughing as hard as I was.

Humphrey didn't show up that day to paint, but that afternoon Pa, Ma, and I drove into town to pick up some supplies. Who should be behind the counter at the general store but Humphrey.

"Sorry I couldn't make it out to paint today, Mr. Stanton," he said. "But Momma's sick in bed, and so's Daddy, so I had to work the counter."

"Humphrey," said Pa, trying his best to compose himself, "I gotta ask you something. What did you paint on my barn?"

Humphrey frowned, trying hard to remember. Then it came to him. "Male Pooch Tobacco," he said, proudly, puffing out his chest, a broad grin stretched across his face.

"Male Pooch?" said Pa. He spelled out the words.

"M-A-L-E-P-O-O-C-H?"

"Yeah," said Humphrey. The grin was gone now, and in its place a frown creased his brow. "I thought that were a little strange, but that's the way Mr. Everingham said it to me. I figured since you got those two nice blue tick hounds, maybe you was goin' into the dog breedin' business."

"And what did you think the word 'tobacco' had to do with breeding dogs?" asked Pa.

"Uh, nothing I guess," replied Humphrey. "But it *is* a

103

tobacco barn."

"It surely is," said Pa, turning away so Humphrey couldn't see him laughing.

"When are you going to finish the rest of the lettering?" I asked.

Humphrey blushed. "Not sure. I cain't remember what else it was Mr. Everingham wanted on there, and he's out of town. Don't know when he'll be back."

"When you hear from him," said Pa, "you ask him to come see me."

It was three days before Mr. Everingham showed up again in Camptown, during which time there'd been a steady stream of people by our place to get a look at the 'Male Pooch' barn, which gave Pa an idea.

"Junior," he said, "let's go into town and see if Howard's still got that canvas he's had stored in his shed."

Sure enough, Mr. McGinnis hadn't gotten rid of it. No one had money to buy canvas.

"Heck, I'll give it to you just to get the dad-burned thing out of here," said Mr. McGinnis. "I need the space for some new supplies I got coming in."

Pa and I loaded the canvas into the wagon and headed back to the farm.

"My lands!" exclaimed Ma, when she came out to see what we were about. "What in tarnation are you fixing to do with that?"

At first, when Pa told her his plan, she told him he was crazy. But then she got to thinking more about it.

"Might work," she said, nodding.

For the next two days, Ma and the girls worked on the canvas, sewing the several medium-sized pieces into one large piece, while Pa and I rigged up a contraption on the outside of the barn. When the canvas was ready, Pa and I hauled it down to the barn and strung it up to the framework we'd constructed.

We stood back, admiring our handiwork and reading the sign Pa had painted on the canvas.

SEE THE ONLY
MALE POOCH BARN
IN KENTUCKY
5 cents

We'd rigged the canvas so it could be easily pulled up using a rope. Pa figured when anyone came by willing to pay a nickel to see the barn, one of us would raise the canvas. Otherwise, it hung down, covering the side of the barn.

A couple of the younger kids said they could set up an iced tea stand there, too.

The day after we hung the canvas, Mr. Everingham showed up.

"What's this?" he demanded.

"Oh, that's right," chortled Pa. "You hain't seen young Mr. McGinnis's handiwork yet, have you?"

When Pa raised the canvas to reveal what Humphrey had painted, poor Mr. Everingham almost had a heart attack.

"Oh, my!" he exclaimed. "This is bloody awful. We must correct this at once! I am so sorry!"

"No, I don't think so," said Pa.

"What do you mean?"

"I kinda like it the way it is," said Pa. "Besides, I'm thinking I can make a little extra money off'n it."

"But, but . . . this is preposterous!" sputtered Mr. Everingham.

"Nevertheless," said Pa, "that's the way it is. Now, here's what I am willing to do. If you want young Mr. McGinnis to

**105**

finish the sign, without changing what's already there, that'd be fine. 'Course, I think that'd just make your company look a little more dumb than it already does."

Mr. Everingham was speechless. He stared at Pa. Then, he walked back to his car, got in, and drove away. We never saw him again.

*****

Pa was right. People *did* pay to see the "Male Pooch" sign.

Oh, we didn't make a fortune off of it—not even close. But the nickels that came in here and there plus the pennies from the iced tea stand were a welcome addition to our family's income over the next year and a half, and more than once was what we used to buy food for our next meal.

Pa and Ma are long dead now, and the farm belongs to some other family. But, occasionally, when I'm back in Camptown, I drive past the place. The old barn's still there, though it's no longer used.

Wind and rain have done their jobs in removing about every bit of evidence of Humphrey's work, and the canvas, as well as all the doors, is long gone, as are most of the letters.

But if you look real close, and the light is just right, you can still barely make out a few remaining letters:

M LE  OOCII

## DOWN IN THE RIVER
## 1943

*As I went down in the river to pray*
*studying about that good old way*
*and who shall wear the robe and crown*
*Good Lord, show me the way!*

*O, brothers let's go down*
*let's go down, come on down,*
*come on brothers let's go down,*
*down in the river to pray.*

Brother Merle Goodman studied the young girl, her eyes closed, her arms uplifted, her words merging with those of the hundred or so other people at the revival meeting that evening. It was a hot night, even for July. Wet circles formed by perspiration stained the underarms of her blouse. He knew his own shirt had the same telltale sign of sweat, easily noticeable when he got to preaching and waving his arms around, the way he did when the spirit moved him.

He'd known Lorelei Johnson all her life. Indeed, he had been the one to preach the funeral service for her mother, who died giving birth to the girl. A miracle, they said, that the baby even survived, the way the umbilical cord was wrapped around its neck.

When she was seven years old and her daddy was killed in a drunken brawl, it was Merle and his wife, Elsbeth, who took her into their home and raised her along with their son and their own three girls, the youngest of which was the same age as Lorelei.

No way would she allow the girl to be put in St. Angeles Orphanage, Elsbeth had declared.

It mattered not to them she was slow—retarded, the doctor from over in Wellspring had concluded. A good girl, she did her chores, minded her manners, and was quick to obey any orders Merle or his wife gave her. She didn't have a particularly pretty face, yet she wasn't homely, either. *Plain* might be the best word to describe her.

Lorelei was about twelve years old when Merle first noticed her body was changing, developing from one of a little girl into a young woman. Almost overnight, it seemed, she had breasts where, before, there was but a skinny little kid. He'd begun to feel a stirring inside himself, an arousal he did his best to subdue through prayer and, when that failed, by going out into the woods behind the house and masturbating.

The Saturday before Lorelei turned fourteen, Merle walked down to the river, running over in his mind what to preach on the next day. He came upon her unexpectedly, standing in the water's shallow part.

She was naked.

Merle quickly ducked behind a bush, so as to not embarrass the girl.

Peeking through the branches, he watched her emerge from the river, his heart pounding as he stared at her body. She looked so young and so perfect.

He hated himself that he didn't have the willpower to walk away. He hated her, too, that she exposed herself like that, and caused him to be tempted.

Shortly after that, a book salesman came through town. Out of curiosity, Merle purchased a book that explained the origin of names, a subject that had always intrigued him. He was surprised to discover that *Lorelei* came from the German, and was the name of a dangerous rock that jutted out into the Rhine. According to legend, a siren perched on the rock, luring ships to their destruction.

*Just like she's trying to lure me*, Merle thought at the time.

Now she was fifteen years old and, though still plain of face, the fullness of her figure no longer left any doubt in anyone's mind she was a grown woman.

*As I went down in the river to pray*
*Studying about that good old way*
*And who shall wear the starry crown*
*Good Lord, show me the way!*

*O sisters let's go down,*
*Let's go down, come on down,*
*O sisters let's go down,*
*Down in the river to pray.*

Merle shook himself from his reverie. The hymn was over. Time for him to deliver his sermon.

For this week-long revival, he'd decided to preach each night on one of the seven deadly sins. Tonight's topic was lust.

The scripture he had chosen was Matthew 5:28.

Merle cleared his throat, then read, "But I say unto you, whosoever looketh on a woman to lust after her hath committed adultery with her already in his heart."

He stole a glance at Lorelei, then launched into his sermon.

109

*****

Following the service, Merle greeted the worshippers as they filed out of the tent, enduring the hugs of the older women and receiving platitudes for the message he'd given that evening.

"Just what some certain people needed to hear." "Ain't it terrible what men gots in their hearts?" "Praise God, Jesus washes away all our sins!"

He nodded, smiled, and shook hands, but his thoughts were elsewhere, specifically on how much of an offering had been received. For while the primary purpose of these twice-a-year revivals was to save souls—and sixteen answered the altar call this night—a very real and important secondary purpose was to augment what Elsbeth seemed to take great pleasure in reminding him was the "pitifully small and woefully inadequate" salary paid him by the Chickapea Baptist Church.

He was surprised when Lorelei came up and wrapped her arms around him, hugging him tightly. Her breasts pressed against him, and he felt a stirring in his loins.

"Brother Goodman, that sure were a good message. I thank Jesus he don't let me have none of those deadly sins. But I know if'n I did, he'd forgive me for them. I love Jesus, and I love you!"

"I love you, too, Lorelei. Now, you best be joining up with Elsbeth and the others, and getting on home." Reluctantly, he removed his arms from around her and stepped back. But she didn't move.

"I'd like to stay awhile if'n I might. I got somethin' to ask you later."

Merle looked puzzled. What did she want that she couldn't ask him at home?

"All right," he said. "Go tell Elsbeth you'll be coming home

110

with me in a little while."

As Lorelei raced off to convey the message, Merle forced himself not to follow her body with his eyes. Instead, he allowed himself a friendly hug and a kiss on the cheek from Mrs. Oldenham. No temptation there: Mrs. Oldenham was eighty if she was a day and her figure, whatever it might have been at one time, had long ago gone south.

*****

It was a pretty good collection: one hundred and twenty-seven dollars and ninety-four cents. Plus, Herman Sachleben had put a note in he'd be bringing a ham over to the parsonage on Thursday.

Merle was about to leave when he remembered Lorelei was waiting for him.

He found her at the back of the tent, spread out on her back on the cool grass, asleep.

For a moment he stood there, looking at her, watching the rhythmic rising and falling of her breasts, breasts so perfectly formed, breasts he longed to touch, to take in his hands, to caress, to place his lips to, sucking the sweet brown nipples he knew without a doubt crowned those two heavenly mounds.

"Jesus Christ," Merle muttered to himself.

What in God's green earth was he thinking? She was a child, the same age as one of his own daughters. She lived in his house *as* his daughter. Besides, he was married. Remember what you just preached to your flock, Merle. Get thee behind me, Satan!

"Lorelei?"

She opened her eyes and looked up.

"Brother Goodman? Oh, I must have fallen asleep."

"You said there was something you wanted to ask me."

She sat up, and he helped her to her feet.

"Yes, sir. I been thinkin', and I reckon it's time I got myself baptized."

Whatever question Merle thought she might have wanted to ask him, this wasn't it.

"You want to be baptized?"

"Yes, sir. I want to be ready for heaven when Jesus calls me."

Merle put his hand to his chin, rubbing it as he pondered the girl's request.

"I s'pose it'd be all right," he said. "You're old enough. Tomorrow morning we'll go over to the church and get you a baptismal gown, and then head on down to the river. I'd ask Elsbeth to come along, but I know she's planning to take the children for a visit to see her aunt over to Crownsville. So, I reckon it'll just be you and me."

"Oh, thank you, Brother Goodman," squealed Lorelei, throwing her arms around his neck.

Merle put his arms around Lorelei and held her tight for a few minutes, reveling in the feel of her body against his. Finally, he let her go. "Come on," he said. "Let's get on home."

*****

"Here," said Merle, handing a white gown to Lorelie. "This should fit you, I reckon."

"Should I put it on now?"

"No, wait 'til we get to the river. You can put it on there."

The Chickapea River was the perfect place for baptizing. Though it was almost a hundred yards wide, one could walk out a good ten yards and still be in water no more than a few feet deep. A number of large boulders formed a little pool near

*As I went down in the river to pray*
*Studying about that good old way*
*And who shall wear the starry crown*
*Good Lord, show me the way!*

O *fathers let's go down,*
*L* *go down, come on down,*
*athers let's go down,*
*in the river to pray.*

en he finished, Merle rose and pulled up his undershorts
ts, then slid the suspenders back up over his shoulders.
ind was racing: *If word of this ever gets out, I'll be ruined!*
lay whimpering on the ground.

ill have to be our secret," said Merle. "No one
now about your sin."

dded, a blank look on her face.

his hand down to her. "Come on, let's get you

t to her feet she spotted the blood on her

s! What is that? What's happened to me?"
aid Merle. "That's just the physical sign of
ed off in the river, just like your sins will."
nd, he led her into the still pool of water,
er knees.

s told, and as she did the blood from
a pinkish color.

le her, placed his right hand behind
b and index finger of his left hand,

ck," he commanded.

6

the shore, where the water was still, not running fast like it did
out in the middle.

"What do I do now?" asked Lorelei, when they reached the
river's edge.

"Go over behind that stand of trees, there," said Merle,
pointing. "Take off all your clothes and put on your gown."

A look of concern crossed Lorelei's face. "*All* my clothes?"

"Don't worry," said Merle. "There's only you and me out
here, and when you get baptized you have to be free of all your
worldly trappings—except the robe. The Lord allows that for
modesty purposes." He glanced at her hair, which she normally
wore in a bun on the back of her head. "Oh, and make sure
you let your hair down, too."

Moments later, when Lorelei stepped out from behind the
trees, Merle stifled a gasp. He had never seen a body as
beautiful as hers! The robe, though loose-fitting, did nothing to
hide the firmness of her fifteen-year-old breasts. If anything, it
accentuated their perfection. He saw the two points where her
nipples pushed out against the smoothness of the fabric. And
with her dark brown hair falling almost to her waist, she
reminded him of the angel in the stained glass window over at
the Baptist Church in Richfield.

Quickly, he regained his composure.

"Now the first thing," he said, "is you have to confess your
sins. Then, I'll baptize you, and your sins will be washed away."

Lorelei's shoulders slumped; she appeared crestfallen. "But
. . . but I don't have no sins," she said.

Tears rolled down her cheeks.

"Nonsense," said Merle, "everybody has sins."

"I don't know what they are, then," said Lorelei, tears
coming harder now.

Merle looked at her and realized she was telling the truth—
she didn't have any sins. At least, none he knew of. And she

113

had lived in his house for the last eight years. It was at that moment his resolve gave way.

"Then I guess we'll have to get you to have a sin. Otherwise, I cain't baptize you, and you cain't get into heaven."

"How will we do that?" asked Lorelei, raising the hem of her gown and wiping the tears from her face, in the process inadvertently exposing her legs to a point slightly above her knees.

Merle couldn't help but notice.

"You and me will have sex," said Merle. "That'll be your sin, and then I can baptize you."

Lorelei's eyes widened. "Sex? You and me? But . . . but won't that be a sin for you, too?"

"Don't make no difference," said Merle, feeling himself beginning to get hard. "I done been baptized, so all my sins are already forgive, the ones I done did, and any I will do. Besides, I'm a preacher, and it's my job to make sure you're ready to get baptized, so you see, it's not really a sin at all on my part, since I'm doing the Lord's work."

The explanation sounded so logical that, for a moment, Merle almost believed it himself.

"Well, I guess it's okay if you put it that way," said Lorelei. "What do I do now?"

"Lay down here on this grassy spot," said Merle, "and pull your gown up around your waist."

Lorelei did as he said.

Merle slid his suspenders off his shoulders and let his pants fall down around his ankles. He slid his undershorts down to join them.

Lorelei's eyes widened again as she stared at Merle's erection.

"Are you going to put that in me?" she asked in a whisper.

"Don't worry," said Merle. "It'll fit."

"Will it hurt?"

"A little, at first, but this here's a sin you're committing, so it should hurt."

Merle knelt down beside her outstretched body, put so spittle on his fingers, and gently began to massage her vulv

"What are you doin'?" asked Lorelei, raising her h see.

"Getting you a little wet so it'll go in easier," said

In one swift movement, he swung his body ov drove himself into her, feeling for a split second of her hymen before it gave way under the thrust. A torrent of blood gushed forth, stain white robe that lay beneath the girl.

Merle plunged deep inside her, as far go, filling her cavity.

"Uunngh!" cried Lorelei, the sou hand over her mouth.

"Quiet!" said Merle. "We don't

He closed his eyes and begar out, feeling the smooth friction free hand, he pulled up the breasts. They were more p Gently, he massaged one began sucking, first one,

Sweat poured dow and from the end of the girl's own perspi

He felt her m participation, he

"Don't worry," said Merle. "It'll fit."

"Will it hurt?"

"A little, at first, but this here's a sin you're committing, so it should hurt."

Merle knelt down beside her outstretched body, put some spittle on his fingers, and gently began to massage her vulva.

"What are you doin'?" asked Lorelei, raising her head to see.

"Getting you a little wet so it'll go in easier," said Merle.

In one swift movement, he swung his body over hers, and drove himself into her, feeling for a split second the resistance of her hymen before it gave way under the pressure of his thrust. A torrent of blood gushed forth, staining the part of the white robe that lay beneath the girl.

Merle plunged deep inside her, as far as he could possibly go, filling her cavity.

"Uunngh!" cried Lorelei, the sound muffled by Merle's hand over her mouth.

"Quiet!" said Merle. "We don't want anyone to hear!"

He closed his eyes and began to move in and out, in and out, feeling the smooth friction of her as he did so. With his free hand, he pulled up the front of her robe, revealing her breasts. They were more perfect than he remembered them! Gently, he massaged one of them. He lowered his head and began sucking, first one, then the other.

Sweat poured down his forehead, dripping from his chin and from the end of his nose, mixing and becoming one with the girl's own perspiration.

He felt her moving beneath him, whether in struggle or in participation, he wasn't sure. Nor did he care.

*As I went down in the river to pray*
*Studying about that good old way*
*And who shall wear the starry crown*
*Good Lord, show me the way!*

*O fathers let's go down,*
*Let's go down, come on down,*
*O fathers let's go down,*
*Down in the river to pray.*

When he finished, Merle rose and pulled up his undershorts and pants, then slid the suspenders back up over his shoulders.

His mind was racing: *If word of this ever gets out, I'll be ruined!*

Lorelei lay whimpering on the ground.

"This will have to be our secret," said Merle. "No one should ever know about your sin."

The girl nodded, a blank look on her face.

He reached his hand down to her. "Come on, let's get you baptized."

As Lorelei got to her feet she spotted the blood on her robe.

"Oh, sweet Jesus! What is that? What's happened to me?"

"Never mind," said Merle. "That's just the physical sign of your sin. It'll be washed off in the river, just like your sins will."

Still holding her hand, he led her into the still pool of water, which came about to her knees.

"Sit down," he said.

Lorelei did as she was told, and as she did the blood from her robe turned the water a pinkish color.

Merle knelt down beside her, placed his right hand behind her head and, with the thumb and index finger of his left hand, pinched her nose shut.

"Close your eyes and lay back," he commanded.

116

When Lorelei was completed immersed, Merle began. "Lorelei Johnson, I baptize you in the name of the Father . . ."

*Can I trust her not to ever tell anyone what happened?*

He raised her back up out of the water and she took a quick breath before being lowered again. ". . . and of the Son . . ."

*After all, she's slow—she could let something slip out without even realizing it.*

Merle raised her a second time for a quick breath, then lowered her again. ". . . and of the Holy Ghost."

This time he didn't raise her.

Instead, with the hand with which he'd been cradling her head, he grabbed her hair, pulling her down to the bottom of the pool. He removed his other hand from her nose, placed it on her breastbone, and pushed down.

Lorelei opened her eyes wide and looked up at Merle. An expression of panic spread over her face, and she began to struggle, grabbing his left wrist in both of her hands, trying to push his hand away. But her fifteen-year-old body proved no match for his forty-seven-year-old one. She kicked her legs in a vain attempt to get up.

Merle swung his body over hers as he had done a few moments earlier when they'd had sex, and pinned her more firmly under the water, his face inches away from the girl's.

Suddenly, he plunged his face beneath the water and kissed her full on the lips.

When he raised his head out of the water, Lorelei's face was frozen in an expression of disbelief.

"I'm sorry," said Merle, almost in a whisper. "I'm sorry."

He continued to hold her down.

After a few minutes, her struggling ceased. Eyes still wide open, she stared vacantly up at Merle.

He got to his feet, dropping his arms to his side. Tears ran down his face and mingled with the river water dripping from

117

his wet hair. He lifted his head heavenward.

"I'm sorry," he said again. "Oh, my God, I'm so sorry! Forgive me, Lord!"

Taking the girl by her arms, he dragged her from the pool, out to where the water rushed rapidly in its course downstream. Once there, he figured, he would slip the robe off of her, and let the river carry her body on its currents. He'd leave her clothes where she had neatly piled them so later when she was found, people would think she'd gone swimming and drowned. He hadn't told Elsbeth about the baptism so there'd be no one to know he'd even been there.

Merle managed to get the body into the main part of the river. As he stepped over it, preparing to remove the robe, it happened.

He fell.

In the split second before his head hit the boulder, he could have sworn a hand reached out and grabbed his ankle.

*O sinners let's go down,*
*Let's go down, come on down,*
*O sinners let's go down,*
*Down in the river to pray.*

*****

From the *Camptown Southern Gazette*
*July 18th, 1943*

### TWO DROWN IN RIVER ACCIDENT

*In what appeared to be an unsuccessful attempt to save a young girl from drowning, Brother Merle Goodman, pastor of the Chickapea Baptist Church, entered life eternal this past Wednesday.*

*According to Sheriff Burleigh Cole, Brother Goodman's body and that of Miss Lorelei Johnson, a fifteen-year-old girl who lived in the Goodman home, was found washed up on the bank of the Chickapea River, some three miles downstream from where Miss Johnson's clothes were discovered, neatly stacked behind a tree.*

*As Miss Johnson was wearing a baptismal robe, Sheriff Cole speculated she was being baptized by Brother Goodman, and something went terribly wrong. It can only be hoped the baptism was accomplished before the accident took place.*

*Services for both victims will be held tomorrow afternoon at three o'clock at the Chickapea Baptist Church. The Reverend Ollie McGowan, pastor of the First Baptist Church of Crownsville, will officiate.*

*According to Mrs. Elsbeth Goodman, Brother Goodman's widow, her husband and Miss Johnson will both be buried in the Goodman family plot at the Chickapea Baptist Church Cemetery.*

## I NEVER SAW THE COLOR BLUE
### 1955

Everyone always did say my sisters and I were an odd lot. They were right.

First of all, we attended the Lutheran Church. This in a town that, as my daddy used to say, had more Baptists than people. It was worse later on when we moved to Camptown, Kentucky, which didn't even have a Lutheran Church. Instead, we attended the Methodist Church, the closest thing we could find.

Both of my parents were very religious. My mother was the supreme optimist. My father's greatest strength was his wonderful sense of humor.

Something else that made my sisters and me collectively odd was our physical disabilities. Now, it's not all that strange to have a family member with a physical disability. But when all three children do, well . . .

I was the oldest. My name is Bonnie. I was born blind.

I never saw the color blue. Never saw a Christmas tree. Never saw my mother's or father's faces. My sisters, twins two years younger than me, are Molly and Dolly. Molly was born mute, Dolly, deaf. My father joked it was like having Helen Keller all rolled into three. We never bothered to tell him Miss Keller was only blind and deaf—not dumb.

My mother, always upbeat and hopeful, had no doubt that what God shorted us in terms of sight, speech, and hearing, he made up for in other ways.

For Dolly's sake, we all learned to use sign language at an early age. I couldn't see what anyone else was "saying," but I could sign with the best of them—or so I was told. I knew sometimes when my sisters didn't want me to know what they were talking about, they'd sign without Dolly doing the verbal translation. I'd get so mad!

While I always wondered what my mother and father, and Molly and Dolly, looked like, most of all I wondered what *I* looked like. I knew I was a little overweight. Okay, more than a little—but not a lot. I had long hair that came down below my shoulders. Beyond that, my appearance was a complete mystery to me. Was I pretty? Ugly? How would I know? How could I tell? My parents always said I was pretty. My sisters always said I was as ugly as a frog. I figured one pair was as biased as the other, but I didn't know which to believe.

The answer came when I was thirteen-years-old.

Five years earlier, when I was eight, and Molly and Dolly were six, our father moved the family from Tennessee to Camptown, where Mother's folks lived. Camptown was the home of Richmond Academy, a school for the physically impaired, where Daddy enrolled my sisters and me. Every Spring the school held a dance in the Camptown High School gymnasium. Although Molly, Dolly, and I learned how to dance from our mother, none of us had ever danced with a boy. Oh, we danced with our father, but he didn't count.

When I was thirteen, I decided I wanted to go to the dance. My mother thought it a wonderful idea, but Molly and Dolly must go with me, she said. While the idea of my two younger sisters tagging along didn't exactly thrill me, I realized having them accompany me was probably not only necessary but could be advantageous in at least one respect: they could let me know which boys were cute and which weren't. Not that I had any illusions any boy might ask me to dance. But . . . just in case.

By the time my father dropped us off at the gymnasium, the dance had already been underway for more than an hour. It had rained earlier, and the air had a clean, fresh, feel and smell to it. I mention this only because of the contrast when we entered the building. One of those "gifts" God gave me to make up for my lack of sight is a keen sense of smell. Inside the gymnasium the air was awash with a multitude of scents and aromas: cologne, hairspray, perfume, aftershave lotion, perspiration, and, from somewhere far off, probably the boy's bathroom or maybe the girl's, a faint trace of cigarette smoke—all in subtle competition with one another for supremacy, and none able to come out on top.

The blaring sounds of *Rock Around The Clock* assaulted our ears and, combined with the gyrations of the couples on what I was sure was a packed dance floor, as well as the clamor of a room full of chattering teenagers, caused the whole place to vibrate: the walls, the floor—including me. I could *feel* the energy.

But what I felt even more was the trembling of my legs, and the knot in the pit of my stomach, symptoms of the panic growing in me since early that morning, when the realization truly struck me I was going to my first dance—and no one would ask me to dance! I was absolutely convinced of it. Who would want to dance with someone who was overweight, and didn't even know if she was cute or not?

As the day wore on I'd become more and more convinced I'd be spending the whole evening with my two *little* sisters, listening while they described the action. I'd even thought about not going, but my mother—*absolutely positive* something wonderful would happen—had insisted. Now that I was actually at the dance, I thought I would consider myself lucky if I didn't throw up, or faint from either nervousness or embarrassment.

The first thing we did was head for the girl's bathroom. My purpose was twofold. First of all, if I did heave all over myself, I wanted to be someplace where I could get cleaned up quickly. But the more practical reason was that it was here Molly and Dolly would apply my makeup.

You see, while my mother was cool in many ways, allowing us girls to wear makeup was not one of them. But there was no way I was going to be at this dance without at least a little lipstick and rouge on. I'd borrowed some from one of the freshmen girls with whom I was friendly, and arranged for my sisters to put it on me when we arrived at the dance, then take it off afterward, before we left for home. I also dabbed a little *Just You* perfume behind my ears.

When the girls finished, I asked them how I looked.

"Fine," said Dolly, in a none too convincingly tone. By this point, I didn't know if I looked like a model or a clown. The latter was my educated guess.

We went back into the gymnasium, got some drinks, and found a place to stand against one wall. I listened while Dolly described the scene before us, shouting in my ear to make herself heard over the din.

She began tugging furiously on my sleeve.

"What is it?" I signed.

"There's a boy coming this way."

My heart jumped! I turned my back so I could sign to Dolly without the boy seeing. "Who is it? Is he cute? Is he going to ask me to dance?"

God, I was so nervous!

"Maybe," said Dolly. "It's Billy Thoreson, I think. And,

yeah, he's okay."

Billy Thoreson. I remembered he was in my English class.

"Hi, Bonnie. Wanna dance?"

I turned back around, nodded, held out my hand and he took it in his. His hand felt smooth and warm. But not sweaty, thank goodness. He led me out to the dance floor and took me in his arms. The band was playing *The Great Pretender*, a nice slow song, for which I was most grateful. Billy held me close, and I smelled the pungent scent of his Old Spice. *Was he old enough to shave?* I wondered. I felt the smooth texture of his suede jacket under my left hand, which rested easily on top of his right shoulder.

"I've seen you in English class," he said.

"You have?" I managed to mumble.

"Yeah. I think you have awful nice hair. And you smell nice, too."

"Thank you."

I didn't know what else to say. Should I tell him he smelled nice? Maybe not.

Billy grasped my right hand a little tighter. "I think you're really cute, too," he said.

The shock from what he said caused me to miss a step, resulting in our feet getting tangled up. We almost fell down.

Billy laughed. "I'm sorry; I didn't mean to fluster you."

"Oh, no, *I'm* sorry," I said. I screwed up all the courage I could muster and asked, "You really think I'm cute? I'm not too fat?"

"Fat? Heck, you're not fat. You're just right. Yeah, I think you're really cute."

"My sisters put my lipstick on me. I probably look like a clown."

I still couldn't believe he thought I was *cute*.

"Gee, I think you look great. Relax. Let's dance."

I danced with Billy Thoreson at least a half dozen more times that evening. And with Harlan Winthrop. And Augie Rafferty. And . . .

*****

At the end of the semester, Billy's family moved to California and I never saw him again. But I'll never forget him, or that special night, when he helped me realize I wasn't ugly nor was I *too* fat; I was *cute*, and a boy could find me attractive.

My mother was right: Something wonderful *did* happen at that dance!

## NUMBERS
## 1958

". . . and to my nephew, Allan Gillespie . . ."

About time, I thought.

I'd been sitting for the better part of forty-five minutes listening to the attorney read my late uncle's will. Up to that point he'd left between fifty and five hundred dollars to about everyone he'd ever known in his life, including the waitress at the restaurant where he always ate breakfast, and the ten-year-old kid who delivered his newspaper—and who could never manage to get it on the porch.

The one exception was his church, St. Timothy Catholic Church, which was the recipient of five thousand dollars.

The only brother of my late mother, Patrick "Paddy" Gilligan O'Brien never married. He'd been what some people might call a curmudgeon; without a doubt the most difficult, nastiest man I'd ever known. I did my best to avoid his company, but for some reason, he seemed to like mine, although I have no idea why.

Every Monday he would have my wife, Joanne, and me, to his house for dinner. He said he didn't mind having company that night, since there wasn't anything worth listening to on the radio anyway. Whenever I grumbled to Joanne about this unwanted imposition on my time she was quick to remind me I was his sole living relative—both of my parents having been killed some years earlier in an auto accident—and it wouldn't hurt me to spend some time with him since he appeared, as I said, to enjoy our company.

Mrs. Goodman, who kept house and cooked for him for the last ten years—she was one of the five hundred dollar recipients—always prepared something special. The food was wonderful, but the entire mealtime was spent listening to my uncle complaining: about the economy; the neighborhood; the price of everything; politics; how the world was going to hell in a handbasket. In fact, the only thing he never complained about was religion.

Okay, he complained about my lack of it, and Joanne's lack of it, as he saw it.

If nothing else, my uncle was a religious man. I would have thought this might have made him a little more loving, but it did not. His attendance at church mirrored mine and Joanne's: he never missed a Sunday; we never made one. Not that we were atheists or anything; we just didn't care much for organized religion.

Besides complaining, it seemed to have been my uncle's sole purpose in life to get Joanne and me into church. He tried everything from pleading to offering us a paid vacation to Myrtle Beach. I never did understand *why* Myrtle Beach. But we weren't interested.

Now, I was sure, he was up in heaven somewhere—yes, okay, I believe he got there—looking down on us—on me—and plotting his next move.

Whereas my parents tried their hand at several different businesses—all of which failed—and died pretty much penniless, Uncle Paddy worked at the same factory job all his life until he retired eight years ago at the mandatory age of sixty-five. He owned the house he lived in but, from the way he'd let it run down, and from the dilapidated state of his furniture, I doubted he had much more to leave than my parents had.

" . . . I bequeath the balance of my estate, consisting of my home located at 157 Tremaine Rd., Camptown, Kentucky, 40300 . . ."

God, he even spelled out the zip code? And I knew this was coming: I *knew* he'd leave me that old run-down place that would require a small fortune to fix up if I had any hope of unloading the damn thing. And for this, I wasted every one of my Monday evenings for the last eight years!

". . . in addition to five hundred thousand dollars in bearer bonds . . ."

I felt Joanne's nails dig into the fleshy part of my hand between the thumb and forefinger. But it didn't seem to faze me. What did I just hear? Five . . .?

". . . provided the following conditions are met."

Then came a pregnant pause as the attorney shifted his eyes from the sheets of paper before him and looked directly at me. His mouth curled up into a little smirk. Not a friendly—*you're going to be happy when you hear this* grin—but rather an expression that said *now here's the part where you get screwed.*

He looked back down at the papers and resumed reading.

"The conditions are these: The bonds are in a safe I own located in the office of my attorney, Richard J. T. Thornton. The safe's combination consists of four numbers, the first being clockwise, the second counterclockwise, and so on. No one knows the combination, including Mr. Thornton. The beneficiary has one week from the reading of this will to ascertain the combination and unlock the safe. The beneficiary may try the combination once, and only once, each day. If he is successful in opening the safe within the allotted time period, the bonds are his. If not, a professional locksmith will be called

128

in to open the safe, and the bonds will become the property of my church, St. Timothy Catholic Church, referenced elsewhere in this will.

"My nephew has always been a puzzle to me. I did not understand why he disliked church so much. I did not understand why he acquiesced to come to my home for dinner every Monday evening when he disliked me so much unless he thought I had money, which I don't believe he did. Ha! Fooled you!"

At this, Mr. Thornton looked up at me and grinned his stupid grin. Then he continued reading.

"Above all, I did not understand his affinity for the Detroit Tigers. But in any event, I have constructed this puzzle for him, if he wishes to be able to open the safe and become a rich man.

"I have already provided two clues: that there are four numbers, and the direction to dial first. Two additional clues are to be found in the sealed envelopes included with this will. From these clues, you should—perhaps, may—be able to figure out the combination. Whether you are successful or not, it is still my fervent hope to someday get you and your lovely wife, Joanne, into church. Good luck, Allan."

Once again Thornton looked up at me as he picked up two envelopes and handed them over. I opened the first. Inside was a slip of paper with a poem written on it:

> *When I was a young man in Paris,*
> *I discovered a book by H. Caris.*
> *It wasn't his real name, of course,*
> *But twisted it offers the source*
> *Of knowledge to make the way sure*
> *Of obtaining the old man's treasure.*

Joanne had been reading the poem along with me. "Was your uncle ever in Paris?" she asked.

I nodded. "Yes. My mother told me once when Uncle Paddy was sixteen he lied about his age and joined the army. He was sent to Europe, and spent about five or six months in Paris."

"Do you know what the poem means?" Joanne asked.

I laughed. "I have no idea," I said, as I opened the second envelope. There was another poem, one more familiar to me.

> *This old man, he played four*
> *He played knick-knack on my door*
> *With a knick-knack paddy-whack give a dog a bone*
> *This old man came rolling home.*

> *This old man he played two,*
> *He played knick-knack on my shoe*
> *With a knick-knack paddy-whack give a dog a bone*
> *This old man came rolling home.*

> *This old man he played three*
> *He played knick-knack on my knee*
> *With a knick-knack paddy-whack give a dog a bone*
> *This old man came rolling home.*

> *This old man, he played one*
> *He played knick-knack on my drum*
> *With a knick-knack paddy-whack give the dog a bone*
> *This old man came rolling home.*

"I know that poem," said Joanne. "It's a song, isn't it? But what does it *mean*?"

"One thing I can tell you," I said. "I hate that song. When I

130

was a little kid, whenever I was around Paddy he'd sing the damned thing. I got pretty tired of him whacking me on my knee and my spine and my head.

"And to answer your question: my guess is the old man is Uncle Paddy. And I'm the goddamned dog he's throwing the bone to! But what I don't understand is why the poem's out of sequence. He has the fourth verse first, then the second and the third, and the first verse is last."

"Those could be the numbers," said Joanne. "Four, two, three, one?"

I shook my head. "I can't believe he'd make it that easy. When can I try the first number," I asked the attorney.

"Right now, if you wish."

The three of us stood, and he led us to a small safe in another room.

"Here it is," he said.

I had no idea how big a safe was required to hold five hundred thousand dollars in bearer bonds, but this one was nowhere near as large as I had imagined.

"That's it?" I asked.

"That's it."

I knelt and put my hand on the dial. It was then I realized that, even if I had the correct combination, I had no idea how many times to turn the dial for each number. But I decided to give it a try, turning the same number of times as the number I was trying: four turns to the right for number four; two turns to the left for number two; three turns to the right for number three; and one final turn to the left for number one.

Nothing.

"I assume you'll be back tomorrow?" asked Mr. Thornton in a way that made me want to stand up and smash him in the mouth.

But I didn't. Instead, I smiled, and said, "You bet. When

would be a good time?"

"I'm here from ten until six. Any time during those hours would be fine."

That evening Joanne and I tried to figure out various combinations based on different numbers: Uncle Paddy's address; his date of birth; his phone number; *my* address; *my* date of birth; *my* phone number. We worked with the old man's social security number. I even tried to come up with something from the date Paddy died.

"How could he have known that in advance?" asked Joanne, when I brought it up.

"I don't know," I said. "But I wouldn't put it past him."

The only thing we decided was that the four, two, three, one combination might stand for the number of turns for each number—whatever they might be.

During the next two days, Joanne and I made daily trips to the attorney's office. Each time my attempt to open the safe proved futile.

The third day had been Uncle Paddy's funeral, a graveside service with the priest from St. Timothy's officiating, a Father O'Kearney. Uncle Paddy made all of his arrangements in advance, so I was surprised there was no marker.

"Where's the marker?" I asked the funeral director.

"It's being prepared now," she said. "We expect it to be set within the next few days. Here."

She handed me a small card.

"What's this?" I asked.

"The grave location."

I looked at the card. It contained Uncle Paddy's name, date of death, and today's date, plus the location: Garden 8, Section 43, row 32, plot 9.

Bingo! He's given me the combination!

I drove like a madman to the attorney's office, Joanne

begging me to slow down and predicting I wouldn't live long enough to get the money even if this *was* the right combination.

I ignored her.

When we reached the office I ran up the stairs, leaving Joanne behind.

"You look expectant," said Mr. Thornton. "Ready to try again, are we?"

"I think I've got it this time," I replied.

But I was wrong. The combination didn't work.

Disgusted, I stormed from the office.

*That old son of a bitch!*

***** 

Days four and five proved no more fruitful than the first three.

The afternoon of day five, two days after Paddy's funeral, we received a message from the cemetery office that the marker had been set.

"Shall we take a run out and see it?" asked Joanne.

"Sure," I said. I wanted to see what the old man had to say about himself.

It was an impressive stone, made of marble. I read the engraving:

> *Patrick "Paddy" Gilligan O'Brien*
> *born June 22, 1885*
> *passed into life eternal*
> *August 15, 1958*

Below that was written:

*To labour, and to be content with that a man hath,*
*is a sweet life*
*but he that findeth a treasure is above them both.*
*Through this the treasures are opened:*
*and clouds fly forth as fowls.*

"Jesus! And he thought *I* was a puzzle!" I exclaimed.

"I take it you have no idea what all of that means," said Joanne.

"Absolutely none."

The next day we tried Paddy's phone number; again, nothing.

One more day to go; one more chance to get half a million dollars.

\*\*\*\*\*

Day seven: the final day. We were at a complete loss as to what combination to try.

On our way to the attorney's office, we ran into a detour. Okay, I thought, this is just putting off the inevitable a little bit longer.

"Look," said Joanne, as we turned onto Market Street. "Isn't that St. Timothy's?"

I looked to where she pointed. She was right. It was Paddy's church.

"It's lovely," said Joanne. "Look at all the stained glass windows. Let's stop and see if we can go in."

*Why not?* I thought.

As luck would have it, Father O'Kearney, the priest who officiated Paddy's service, was working in the front yard. He invited us in, said he'd be happy to show us around.

The first place he took us to was a magnificent stained glass window depicting Jesus as a young boy working alongside his father in a carpentry shop.

"Your uncle donated this window," said the priest.

I looked at the inscription at the bottom of the window:

> *To labour, and to be content with that a man hath, is a sweet life:*
> *but he that findeth a treasure is above them both.*
> *Sirach 40:18*
> *Through this the treasures are opened: and clouds fly forth as fowls.*
> *Sirach 43:14*

My mouth fell open.

"That's the same inscription that's on your uncle's marker," said Joanne.

I nodded, dumbly.

"Sirach?" I said. "I've never heard of that book in the Bible. Not that I'm an expert."

"It's in the Catholic Bible, but not the Protestant one," said Father O'Kearney. "In the Protestant Bible, it's one of the intertestamental books, written between the Old and New Testaments. Your uncle said these were his favorite verses."

Father O'Kearney continued showing us the rest of the sanctuary, explaining the background behind the numerous other stained glass windows, and the myriad artifacts every Catholic Church seems to attract.

"And this," he said, leading us through a side door that took us outside, "is our meditation courtyard."

We walked out into a beautiful little garden, shaded by a huge oak tree in the middle of it. Around the tree were several concrete benches where, I assumed, people sat while they meditated. I sat down on one that happened to face the outside of my uncle's window—and almost fell off of it at what I saw!

"Sirach," spelled backward, was "hcariS!" H. Caris! This was what my uncle meant in the poem by saying if you "twisted" the name you find the source.

"Come on!" I grabbed Joanne's hand and ran back into the church, leaving the priest standing alone outside with his mouth open.

"What?" she cried.

I raced us back to the window: 40, 18, 43, 14.

Pulling Joanne behind me I bolted to the car. Within ten minutes we were at the attorney's office. During the brief ride, Joanne kept asking what was going on. My reply was to tell her to wait and see.

"Ah, here for the final try, are we?" asked Thornton, in that sneering tone I had come to detest.

I brushed by him and headed straight to the safe where I knelt and took the dial in my hand.

Forty, four times to the right. Eighteen, twice to the left. Forty-three, three times to the right. One final turn back to fourteen—where the dial stopped on its own.

I turned the handle and the safe door swung open.

My hand trembling, I reached in and brought out what proved to be the first bundle of bearer bonds worth five hundred thousand dollars.

And I said a silent prayer of thanks that my uncle had finally succeeded in getting me into church.

## FULL COURT
## 1962

"My God, they're still there!"

I stopped the car and looked up at the rusted, metal goal attached to the back of the old, gray shed. The front of the rim hung down a good two inches from the back, the result, no doubt, of someone, at some time, hanging there, suspended in space. There was no net. But there hadn't been one when I played here, either.

I say "they" because a little further down the alley, two houses ahead, I saw the other goal, also sans net, but a tad more level than this one, on the garage of my old home.

"*What's* still there?" asked my aunt, who was with me.

I was in Camptown for my fifteenth high school reunion, the first time I'd been back since I left to go to college. I'd taken Aunt Mildred to lunch and, on a whim, decided to drive by the house where I spent the better part of my childhood. After slowly cruising down the street where it was located, I decided to go up the alley behind it to see if anything had changed.

"The goals," I said, "the basketball goals. They're still there."

"The basketball goals? Is there something special about them?"

"No," I said.

But even as the words left my mouth I knew there was. There was something very special about them.

*****

I was four years old when my mother died.

Five years later my father married Grace, a woman who attended the church where he was the pastor. She was a widow with two daughters, one eleven, the other twelve, and we moved into their house.

It was a nice house, I suppose, and my stepmother and stepsisters treated me okay. But for some reason, I never felt like I belonged there, like it wasn't "my" place. The one saving grace was the basketball goal in the alley, mounted on the back of our garage, placed there, I supposed, by some former residents, since the only thing about basketball that interested my stepsisters were the boys who played it on the teams at the schools they attended.

As soon as we got all our things unpacked that first day we moved in, I grabbed my ball and headed for the alley. I'd been shooting around for about five minutes when I saw this kid coming down the alley toward me, dribbling a basketball.

"Hi," I said.

"Hi," he replied. "I'm Roger. What's your name?"

"Les."

"Les? That's a stupid name!"

I felt my face flush.

"It's short for Leslie," I said, somewhat annoyed.

"That's even stupider."

At that point I did what any red-blooded, American kid would do—I punched Roger right in the stomach.

"Oof," he grunted, doubling over and grabbing his middle.

Before I knew what happened, he charged me and knocked me to the ground.

For the next ten minutes, we wrestled around until, exhausted from our efforts, we both stopped—and started giggling.

"You're okay," said Roger.

"Yeah, you're okay too," I replied.

"You wanta play some basketball?" asked Roger, getting up from the dirt.

"Sure."

And that was the beginning of our friendship.

*****

Although Roger was a year younger than me, he was already a good two inches taller. Nevertheless, I more than held my own when it came to basketball. Four more years passed before he could beat me consistently. Even then, we continued to play, and he'd give me "points" to keep the game competitive.

Roger lived two houses away from me, and it was his shed that held the second goal. Rather than be content to play at one basket, we played "full court," racing up and down the alley from shed to garage, and back again.

After our third game that first day, Roger asked if I wanted to walk to the dairy and get an ice cream cone.

That was my introduction to Alamander's Dairy, a veritable cornucopia of ambrosial treats, like milkshakes and ice cream cones of every conceivable flavor. My favorite was Lemon Custard; Roger's was Butter Pecan. They sold other dairy products like cottage cheese, milk, eggs, cream. But it was the ice cream and shakes we were interested in. Later on, when Roger and I were in high school, we both worked at the dairy, dipping those same cones, and mixing those same shakes.

And so, we became best friends. All through grade school we played together almost every day.

At the side of Roger's house was a huge mulberry tree, our favorite place to hang out. I couldn't count the hours we spent there playing "little things," so-called—by us—because our toys were little cars and people and buildings. When our parents asked us what we were playing we'd tell them "lieutenant." Lieutenant, get it? "LT"—little things? We were embarrassed to tell them the truth.

While we *were* best friends, that didn't mean we always got along.

I still vividly remember the day Roger got pissed off at me. I always kept my "little things" in a big box at his house. This particular day, after one of our "disagreements," I went home. Soon I saw Roger coming down the alley carrying my box. When he reached my fence, he flung the whole shooting match over it, scattering toys everywhere. It was a good week before we spoke to one another again.

I remember the good times too, even the summer I broke my right arm playing softball.

All the time my arm was in a cast Roger encouraged—okay, pushed—me to learn to throw with my left arm. Even when he said I looked like a girl throwing, I kept at it, and today I'm pretty ambidextrous.

At seventeen I graduated from high school, and that fall enrolled at a college more than a thousand miles from Camptown. Roger was going to be a senior in high school.

Now, at this point, my story could have several possible endings. One: I go away to college and Roger and I never see one another again. Two: Roger and I remain best friends forever.

Our story has a little bit of both of those scenarios.

After Roger graduated from high school, he enrolled at the same college I was attending. He was there on a basketball scholarship and, as it happened, I was on the cheerleading squad.

Fast forward now to the end of my senior year.

I graduate, and the next day Roger and I get married!

*****

Twelve years later, we've come a long way from the days when we played full-court basketball up and down the alley behind our houses.

We now live in a beautiful home in the country, located on twenty-eight acres of woods. The Chickapea River lies fifty yards from our front door. The only thing missing is—there's no alley behind the house.

But there is a beautiful basketball court Roger had installed out by the garage. It's a first-class court, with goals at each end, foul lanes, free throw lines, and a centerline painted on the surface.

We now have four children: two girls—nine and ten—and eight-year-old twin boys. As I write this I look out my kitchen window and watch my children playing basketball, the girls against the boys. Right now the boys are a smidgen taller than their sisters, and I know all too well that in a few years the girls will be no match for them. For now, though, I feel a certain sense of pride, of female superiority, that the girls are better, and that they're winning!

Yay! Just like it used to be with Roger and me!

# HOPE
## 1968

"That's her, over there by the tree. That's Hope."

I hadn't known what to expect when I first arrived at St. Angeles Home for Orphaned Girls. Still didn't. It seemed impossible my late sister's daughter, my niece, had lived here all these years, unbeknownst to anyone in my family.

When I received the call from the police three days earlier that Mary Lou committed suicide—hanged herself from a rafter in the old barn that sat on our family estate in Long Island—I hadn't been too surprised. Saddened, yes. But not surprised.

For the last ten years or more she had not been the same girl I'd grown up with. Gone was the winsome smile, the sparkling eyes, the way she tossed her head in that carefree manner of hers. In her place was a morose, subdued, reclusive stranger who seemed unable to have, or express, any emotion; a woman whose very existence came to rely on drugs to get her up in the morning, put her to bed at night, and keep her going in between.

What *had* surprised and shocked me was the three-page note she left. Oh, not the part about "life not being worth living," "I might as well be dead," etcetera, etcetera. She expressed those sentiments to me more than once on the rare occasions we managed to hold rational conversations, though I never took her seriously—wishing now I had. What I was *not* prepared for was the last page, her confession of the baby she bore out of wedlock some twelve years earlier, an event she successfully hid from everyone in the family, including me, her only sister, with whom she had, I thought, shared everything; and of how, two days after her daughter's birth, she left her on the steps of St. Angeles Orphanage in a little town called Camptown, somewhere in Kentucky. Lord, I never knew Mary Lou had ever been further east or south than Baltimore! What took her to *Kentucky*?

*Hope* was the name pinned to the baby's blanket. And, in one final attempt to assuage her guilt, the note acknowledged, she purchased a rag doll which she left next to the child.

Those three meager scraps of information—a name, a doll, and an approximate age—were enough for the orphanage to identify the child when I inquired. Yes, they said, she was still there; no, she had never been adopted.

Now, here I was, to reclaim a part of my family that, until three days ago, I never knew existed.

Sister Martin met me when I arrived and took me to find Hope.

I looked to where I thought she pointed. A group of six or seven girls was gathered under a large oak tree, playing their version of *Ring Around The Rosie*.

"Which one is she?" I asked.

The Sister looked at me, then at the group of girls.

"Oh, not them," she said. "Over there, by *that* tree; the one by herself."

This time I followed her finger more carefully. I saw the tree but, at first, nothing else.

Then I saw her.

She sat on the ground, scrunched up so close against the

base of the tree she seemed almost to be an extension of its roots. The morning, bright and sunny, along with the brilliant green expanse of grass that made up the vast grounds of the institution, provided a startling contrast to the dull, gray, lump huddled next to the tree. Had I not been expecting to see a human being there, I'm not sure I would have recognized the figure as such.

I walked toward her. As I got closer I was struck by how tiny and frail she looked. At twelve years of age, she was four to six years older than the other girls who called St. Angeles home, although one would not have guessed that from her appearance. Most of the girls, I was told, were adopted by the time they reached nine or ten. Over the years many couples briefly considered Hope, but none wanted to take her.

Sister Martin had cautioned me to approach her from the front since she was wont to be startled by anyone coming up on her from behind, or from out of her line of sight.

I stopped a few feet away from her. She still didn't look up, although I knew she must have been aware of my presence. She clutched a rag doll to her undersized chest as she gently rocked back and forth. Her shaved head—there'd been a recent plague of head lice, Sister Martin had explained—gave her the appearance of an inmate of a World War II Nazi concentration camp.

"Hello, Hope," I said, in my most reassuring voice.

No response.

I bent down, trying to catch her eye.

"Hello, Hope," I said again, this time more gently than before.

"Hullo."

The word came out flat, dull, like a lump of coal, with no hint of either emotion or curiosity. Still, she did not look up.

"Can you tell me how old you are?"

144

I knew perfectly well how old she was, but anything to get a conversation.

"I dunno."

"How are you today?" I wasn't through trying yet.

"Fine."

The same "blah" lack of any feeling.

I remained silent for a few moments as I studied her—this niece child of mine, this small being who carried in her veins the blood of my sister, my parents, my grandparents—plopped down before me, cross-legged, her bald head downcast, her seemingly single purpose in life that of hugging her doll. For the first time, I noticed her clothes: a plain skirt and blouse; a long-sleeved sweater that lay carelessly unbuttoned down the front; ankle socks; and heavy shoes that seemed more suited for a combat soldier than for a child. The skirt, sweater, and socks were all a grayish color—they reminded me of the ashes in my fireplace at home—their achromatic blandness offset but slightly by the dingy whiteness of her blouse and the unpolished blackness of her shoes.

"Do you know who I am? Did Sister Martin tell you I was coming?"

A negative shake of her head.

"I'm your aunt Marcy, your mother's sister."

She looked up at me, straight into my eyes, and said very definitively, "I don't have a mother. I never had a mother."

She looked back down.

At first, I was stunned. Not so much by her answer—though it was delivered with a force I had not anticipated—but by her face. Like her clothes, it too seemed to totally lack any color. The light pink-toned skin I was accustomed to seeing in others was supplanted in her by the same drab gray as the shading of her clothes. Even her pupils, which I thought might be blue, like Mary Lou's, at first glance seemed to be devoid of

145

all pigment, colorless as water. Then I noticed there *was* a hint of color in the large, empty, eyes staring back at me: green. Pale green, but green nonetheless.

Recovering my senses, I sat down next to my niece and took one of her hands in mine. She resisted me at first, but after a few moments relaxed. I spent the next half hour telling her about the family she never knew: of her mother, my sister; of my husband, George, and our two children, her cousins; her grandfather, my father, who was still living; and her uncle Bill and his wife, and their four children—more cousins. Of her father, I could tell her nothing.

When I finished, she asked me in a voice so small I strained to hear her, "Have you come to take me away?"

My heart leaped! Yes, I told her, this was my express purpose in coming here.

"To the other side?"

"To the other side?" I said. "The other side of what?"

"The other girls say when you've been here too long, and they want to get rid of you, someone comes and takes you away to the other side, and you never come back. If you've been good you go to be with Jesus." She looked disconsolately down at her shoes. "And if you haven't . . ." She didn't finish the sentence. "Where are you taking me?"

I could hold back the tears no longer. They came streaming down my cheeks, ruining, I was sure, the mascara so fastidiously applied a few hours earlier.

"Honey," I said between sobs, "I'm taking you home with me. You're going to live in my house."

Hope looked at me again, a look that said more eloquently than any words could have expressed: *I don't believe you.*

"It's true. You're going to be my little girl now."

When she spoke again I detected, for the first time, a glimmer of hope in her voice.

"And will you be my mother?"

I nodded. I was beyond being able to speak. Still holding her hand, I got to my feet. She rose with me and we started toward the main building. We'd gone but a few yards when I remembered the rag doll still lying under the tree.

"Hope, your doll," I said gesturing.

She let go of my hand and walked back to where the doll lay and with a motion that would have made a placekicker for a professional football team proud, booted the doll as hard as she could, sending it flying into a nearby stand of dense bushes.

Turning, she walked back to me, took my hand, looked up, and for the first time, a smile crossed her face.

"I'm ready," she said.

## SISTER MARTIN
## 1970

It was my usual morning routine: pour a cup of coffee, then open the newspaper to the obituaries to see if anybody I knew died during the previous twenty-four hours.

As pastor of the Chickapea Baptist Church, I liked not to be surprised if Mrs. Bailey called asking, "Pastor Young, did you know Mrs. 'So and So' passed away last night?"

"Yes, Mrs. Bailey," I could reply, "I am aware of that."

There'd been too many times the first few years of my ministry when Mrs. Bailey seemed to take a perverse pleasure in being the one to break the sad news to me of someone's demise, always leaving me with the feeling that, somehow, I failed the deceased in not knowing they had gone to meet their maker. Hell, often the person wasn't even a member of my congregation!

But today was different.

Because the name that jumped out at me, while not one of my members, was someone I once had a close relationship with—too close, I'm afraid.

Tears sprang to my eyes as I read the name again:

*April May Rafferty.*

*News has been received that Miss April May Rafferty (Sister Martin), a native and former resident of Camptown, entered life eternal on*

148

*March 15th in Pittsburgh, Pennsylvania, where she resided for the past twenty-three years. A nun in the Catholic Church, Sister Martin, served as the Administrative Director of an orphanage in Pittsburgh. From 1968 to 1970 she served at St. Angeles Orphanage in Camptown. Additional information will be printed in tomorrow's edition of the Gazette as it is received from Miss Rafferty's brother, Augustus, who still resides in the area.*

I laid the paper down and looked around to see if Sally, my wife, was close by. I didn't want her to find me crying, and have to explain why. I took out my handkerchief, wiped the tears from my eyes, and blew my nose. I removed my wallet and took out the photograph that, unbeknownst to my wife, I'd been carrying for the past quarter of a century.

It seemed like only yesterday.

∞

In the fall of 1969 I was a newly ordained Southern Baptist minister, called to serve my first parish: Chickapea Baptist Church, in Camptown, Kentucky, my home church, and the one where my grandfather, the Reverend Merle Goodman, after whom I was named, served a quarter of a century earlier, until his death in a drowning accident.

I was excited—and scared.

I wondered if my years of training at the seminary in Louisville had prepared me to be the spiritual leader of a group of people, most of whom were thirty to forty years older than I, and who knew me as a snotty-nosed kid growing up in the church. My grandmother and my aunt and her family still attended there.

At least they won't have to call me Father, I thought, like those poor Catholic priests.

I had been on the job two months when I received a call

from Jim Tolbert, pastor of the Camptown Methodist Church, asking if I would consider serving on the board of the local interfaith food pantry. I'd been looking for a way to be more involved in the community, so I said yes. Jim told me the next meeting was Tuesday night. I told him I'd be there.

You could fit about three Chickapea Baptist Churches inside Jim's church, so when I arrived it took me a while to find my way to the room where the meeting was to be held. I like to be on time, even early, for things, so I felt embarrassed to find myself late and the last one to arrive.

Jim introduced me around: Oscar Sternman, pastor of the Nazarene Church; Norville Black, pastor of St. Mark's Episcopal; and Father Eugene O'Kearney, the priest at St. Timothy's Catholic Church. The final board member, a nun, was engrossed in writing something on a legal pad and didn't bother to look up until Jim came to her.

"And this is Sister Martin," said Jim. "Sister Martin serves at St. Angeles Orphanage."

When Sister Martin raised her head and looked at me I felt my breath leave my body. She was the most beautiful woman I had ever seen!

"Welcome, Reverend Young," she said, offering me her hand. "We're all very happy you can join us."

I took her hand in mine, still taken aback not only by her beauty but the sensuousness—completely unintended, I was sure—of her voice.

"As am I, Sister," I said. *As am I.*

It didn't take long to find out that being a board member meant volunteering my time to help stock shelves and fill and hand out sacks of groceries to needy families and individuals who stopped by each afternoon when it was open.

Often, I found myself working alongside Sister Martin.

I discovered from our conversations that, like me, she was

born in Camptown where she attended St. Timothy's until she went away to school. It was Father O'Kearney who suggested she enter the sisterhood. Her parents and two sisters still lived on their farm out in the country. An older brother, who was married, lived in town.

Although she was two years younger than I, we didn't know each other growing up, with me attending the public school and she the Catholic school.

I never knew a nun before, and I was curious about many things: the habits they wore; how they came by their church names—like, Sister *Martin*? And, perhaps most important to me, why they chose to forego marriage and a family to become nuns.

I say, most important to me because I knew I was falling in love with Sister Martin.

One day, when there were just the two of us sorting and shelving the canned goods that had come in, I asked her what her real name was.

"I mean before you became Sister Martin."

She laughed and said, "April May. April May Rafferty."

Which in turn made me laugh.

"April May?" I said.

"I know, I know," she said, smiling. "You see, my mama comes from the hill country over in Eastern Kentucky, where they put a lot of stock in mountain lore. She married Papa when she was really young, and he brought her back here to Chickapea County. When she first got pregnant with my brother, Augie, she went to an old woman who lived in a shack out on Lawson's Creek. My mama wanted to know what she should name the new baby when it came. My mama puts a lot of stock in people's names. Well, the old woman told my mama she should name the baby for the month in which it was born."

151

"That would be August I'm guessing," I said, laughing, remembering she told me her brother's full name was Augustus.

"That's right. So when I was due, she went back to the old woman, who told her the same thing: name me for the month in which I was born.

"That seemed easy enough. The only problem was, the night I was born—and I was born at home, out on the farm—a big storm came up, and the electricity went out. It was April 30th. I was born right around midnight, and without electricity, Mama didn't know for sure what time I was born. She wasn't sure if it was *before* midnight—which would have made me born in April—or after midnight, in which case I would have been born in May. So Mama decided to play it safe and name me after both months: April May."

"And your other two sisters?"

"June was born in June. The last baby was born in December."

"What did she name that one?"

"Donna."

"Donna?"

"Yeah, Mama said she'd be damned if she named one of her babies December."

I laughed again, and she smiled.

And I kissed her.

It was a quick kiss, not passionate or anything, but on her lips. What went through my head that caused me to do what I did, I don't know.

Quickly she stepped back, a surprised look on her face. In a quiet voice, she said, "Why did you do that?"

"I'm sorry," I said. "I don't know what got into me."

"I have to go," she said.

She walked from the room, leaving me standing there

kicking myself for being such an ass.

I didn't see April May again for another week. I'd thought about calling or going out to the orphanage to apologize, but I figured she'd be happy to never see or hear from me again. That's why I was surprised when I got the phone call.

"Reverend Young?"

I recognized her voice immediately.

"Sister Martin?"

"Yes. I need to speak with you."

I felt a knot in my stomach, the same feeling I get whenever I know I've screwed up and am about to get called out over it. Was she going to tell Jim or Father O'Kearney? *Had* she told one of them already? I guessed not, not yet at least. Otherwise, it would be one of them calling me, rather than her.

"All right," I said. "When would you like to meet? And where?"

"There's a little restaurant in Crownsville: *Harold's*. Do you know where it is?"

"Yes."

"Can you meet me there at five?"

"All right."

*****

I didn't recognize her at first without her habit. She wore blue jeans and a floppy wool sweater that did its best, without success, to hide the curves of her breasts. Her hair, an auburn hue that reminded me of the caramel corn Mr. Jepson sells every year in his booth at the county fair, fell in graceful folds down to her shoulders. If I thought she was attractive before, when all I saw was her face, now I could appreciate how stunningly beautiful she truly was.

She came over to the booth and slid in across the vinyl

cushion.

"Why did you do it?" she asked.

"Why did I do what?"

I was stalling. I knew exactly what she was talking about, but I wasn't sure how to answer her.

And she knew I knew what she was talking about, too.

"You know what. Why did you kiss me?"

I looked down at the table. I looked out the window. I looked over at the counter where the waitress, whom I hoped would rescue me by coming to take our order, did a good job of ignoring me. Finally, I looked at April May.

"I'm sorry," I said.

"That's not good enough," she said. "I want to know why you kissed me."

I took a deep breath and let it out. "Because I'm in love with you," I said.

"I was afraid you would say that," she replied.

"But it won't happen again," I quickly assured her.

"Why? Because you don't love me anymore?"

I didn't say anything. No, I definitely had not stopped loving her. Never would, I was sure.

"You frightened me," she said.

"Oh, God, I'm sorry," I said, "I didn't . . ."

"You frightened me," she continued, ignoring my attempt at an apology, "because I realized I'd been wanting you to kiss me. And after you did, I wanted to kiss you back."

I sat back, stunned by her words.

We sat there without saying anything for a few minutes. Now I was grateful the waitress *was* ignoring us.

"So, what now?" I asked, finally.

"I want to know what it's like," she said softly, her eyes now glued to the menu in front of her.

"Know what what's like?" I asked.

154

She looked up at me. "I want to know what it's like to have a man make love to me. I want to know what it's like to have *you* make love to me."

If I thought I was stunned before, I was *really* stunned now.

"I . . . I don't know what to say," I stammered.

"Will you?" she asked.

I smoothed my hair back, trying to decide how to answer her. I wanted to make love to her. But she was a nun. And I was a minister.

"Are you sure?" I asked.

"Yes," she said, more softly than before.

*****

Together with my brother, Eldred, I own a fishing cabin out on Lawson's Creek which our parents left us when they died. When they were still alive, they would take us out there on Sunday afternoons in the summer, after church. Dad and Eldred and I would fish, while Mother read her book. After dinner, we'd usually drive back into town for the evening service. But sometimes we'd pass on church, and stay at the cabin until it was dark enough for us boys to capture lightning bugs to place in a mason jar, with a lid with little holes in it so the bugs wouldn't die. Of course, they always still died.

With Eldred living now in Hawaii, I had the cabin all to myself. I'd usually go out there on Saturday afternoons to work on my sermon for the next day.

That's where I took April May.

It was dark when we pulled up to the cabin. There was no electricity, and the sole source of heat was the fireplace. I quickly got a fire started.

"I'm afraid I don't have anything to eat or drink," I said, remembering we left the restaurant without ordering, which got us a knowing look from the waitress.

"That's okay," said April May. "I'm not hungry—or thirsty."

I debated whether or not we should use the bedroom, but decided since it would take a while for it to warm up, and the living room was already nice and cozy from the fire, we should stay where we were.

I got four blankets from the closet and spread them out in front of the hearth. For a few moments, we both hesitated, staring at one another, not sure what to do next. Then she walked over to me, put her arms around my neck, and kissed me. Kissed me hard. And yet, her lips were soft. I kissed her back.

The next thing I knew we were under the blankets, reveling in the touch of each other's bodies. After we finished, we lay together for a long time, holding each other.

"So, how was it?" I asked, at last.

"Better than I could have imagined," she said, turning her head to me and kissing my nose, "much better."

*****

Over the next six months, we got back to the cabin whenever possible, usually every couple of weeks. I could tell, though, that April May was becoming increasingly troubled over something. I was afraid I knew what. And I was right.

"What's bothering you?" I asked one evening, after a particularly passionate round of lovemaking. "I know something is."

She hesitated for a minute, then said, "Being with you. Like this. It's wrong. I've broken my vows. I've sinned. And so have you."

Her eyes were moist with tears.

I cradled her in my arms. "I know," I said. "It bothers me, too, this not being honest. April May, I love you. I want to marry you. Would you be willing to leave the sisterhood and be my wife?"

She burrowed her head deeper into my chest. "I . . . I don't know."

We didn't say anymore. After we got dressed I drove her back to her car and went home.

*****

Thursday was the regular day for April May and for me to work at the food bank. When I arrived about one o'clock I was surprised to see Jim Tolbert there. Friday was his regular day.

"Jim," I said, "surprised to see you here today. What's up?"

"You haven't heard?" he asked.

"Heard what?"

"Sister Martin. She transferred to an orphanage in Pittsburgh. She's not going to be helping out anymore."

I felt my knees go weak. Fortunately, I was standing by the kitchen counter. I leaned back against it to steady myself. "No, I hadn't heard," I managed to get out. "Kind of sudden, wasn't it?"

"From what Eugene tells me, she went to the Mother Superior out at St. Angeles yesterday and asked to be transferred as soon as possible. It so happened, there was an opening in Pittsburgh. Sister Martin left on the 10:05 this morning."

I was shaken, but somehow I managed to get through the afternoon. Thankfully, there wasn't a whole lot of work to do, so I asked Jim if he minded if I left a little earlier than usual.

The next day I received the letter in the mail.

April May explained that, as much as she loved me, she

realized she had a greater love—for God, for Jesus, and for the church. It wasn't possible, she wrote, for her to stay in Camptown, as she wasn't sure she possessed the willpower not to continue seeing me.

She wouldn't be contacting me again, she ended, and hoped I might forgive her for leaving as she did; and that I could find someone I would love and be happy with the rest of my life.

That was the last contact I ever had with her.

∞

I did fulfill her hope about meeting someone else. Two years after April May left Camptown, I met Sally, newly hired as a teacher at Camptown High School.

We'd dated, fallen in love, gotten married, and had four children, three of whom were still at home. And I did love her, loved her dearly.

But what she would never know, what I could never tell her, was that the one true love of my life, my soul mate, was a young nun whom I had known for less than a year.

I picked up the photograph and the paper and walked down the stairs to the basement where an old coal-burning furnace still heated the parsonage in which Sally and I lived, where *I* had lived since returning to Camptown in 1969.

I opened the furnace door and threw the paper into the roaring blaze. Then I threw in the photograph as well.

As tears streamed down my cheeks, I watched as the picture was quickly consumed by the fire.

*I'll never forget you, April May Rafferty*, I said softly to myself. *Never.*

## ROLLING PINS, QUINCE PIES, AND THE DEVIL'S PLAYGROUND
## 1973

It was the first dead body I'd ever seen.

I'd seen dead bodies in movies and on TV, but this was the first real dead body I'd ever seen in person.

The year was 1973 and I was eleven years old. My daddy, who sold pre-need funeral plans and cemetery plots, won an all-expense-paid trip to Hawaii from his company. Unfortunately, it was only for my parents and didn't include me. Putting me on a train from our home in Kansas City, they shuffled me off to spend my Christmas vacation with my grandmother in Camptown, Kentucky.

To be honest, I didn't mind. Grandpa, who at one time been the county sheriff, died before I was born, so I never knew him. But Mom and Dad and I had been to visit Grandma for a week or two every summer for as long as I could remember, in addition to either Thanksgiving or Christmas each year. We would have all been here this Christmas, if not for my parents' trip.

I liked Grandma. She smelled good, like cookies baking in the oven—which they usually were. My grandma was a really good cook. She could cook like nobody's business!

Whenever we'd come, whether at Thanksgiving or

Christmas, Grandma always baked my favorite pie: quince. I didn't know anyone else who made quince pies, probably because you couldn't find quinces just anywhere or any time of year. It was only from about September through December you could get them, and then only if there hadn't been an early freeze.

There were two quince trees in the whole town. One was on the grounds of St. Angeles Orphanage. The other was in Grandma's backyard.

Camptown was a neat old town. I'd always been fascinated by the statue of a turkey on Main Street in front of one of the antique stores. Grandma told me it was in honor of a turkey that saved a little baby from a cougar. She never told me how the turkey did that, though. She said the statue was life-size, which I always kind of doubted since I'm a little over five feet and it was only about a foot shorter—which I find pretty darn tall for a turkey.

Anyway, here we were on my second day in town, at the Baptist Church, to pay our last respects to Diggy McNamara.

Her real name wasn't Diggy. I knew because on the sign in front of the church were the words "Funeral today – Eulacinda McNamara". Later, when we were inside, I saw another sign with the same name.

And I'm not sure how I was paying my last respects, since I never met Diggy McNamara and had therefore never paid my first respects.

Truth be told, I didn't want to go to the funeral. But Grandma insisted.

"It's important for you to see all of life," she said, "both the livin' part *and* the dead part. Besides," she continued, "Diggy McNamara was an important person in the life of this town, in *my* life, in *your* life, and she deserves our presence at her funeral."

160

I wasn't sure how Diggy McNamara could have been an important person in my life since, like I said, I'd never met the woman, but it was apparent a lot of other people felt like my grandma did because there were people everywhere. In fact, we had a hard time making our way through the crowd gathered on the lawn outside the front door: women in groups, talking; men in their own groups, smoking their cigarettes and cigars. In between and around everyone, little kids scampered like monkeys. And everybody was dressed in black.

"She must have had a big family," I said.

Grandma chuckled. "Nope. She didn't have no family at all—leastways not what you'd call an actual family."

A tall, good-looking man met us at the door. He, too, wore a black suit.

"Mrs. Cole," he said, putting out his hand to Grandma.

"Brother Young," said Grandma.

"A glorious day for a funeral," said Brother Young.

"Indeed it is," said Grandma. "A wonderful day for Diggy to make her journey. Praise be to God! Brother Young, you remember my granddaughter, Katherine?"

"I do," said Brother Young, offering me his hand. "Welcome back to Camptown, Miss Cole."

We entered the church to find it almost as crowded as the front lawn. Except here, nobody was smoking and all the talking was in hushed tones. The small children were all held firmly in hand by either their mother or father—not tearing around like the ones outside.

A group of women converged on Grandma, leaving me to wander about on my own. I came across a wall with a lot of photographs hanging on it, all men and all with very serious faces. The first one was of Reverend Young. The plaque below it read:

161

*Reverend Merle Young*
*1969 –*

Further down I saw another photo of a man who looked a lot like Reverend Young. The plaque below that one read:

*Reverend Merle Goodman*
*1923 – 1943*

"That's Brother Young's grandfather."

I looked up to see one of the women who had been talking with Grandma standing next to me.

"I thought I saw a resemblance," I said.

"Tragic, the way he died;" said the woman, "trying to save a young girl from drowning down in the Chickapea River. But they both perished—terrible shame."

The woman introduced herself as Mrs. Bailey. She already knew who I was.

"Your grandmother said she's ready to go see the body now."

I nodded and followed as she led the way to where Grandma was still talking with the other women. She took my hand and we walked into the sanctuary and down the middle aisle to where a casket sat in which rested whom I presumed to be the late Diggy McNamara.

Other than the sight of a dead body, which, as I said earlier, was the first one I'd ever seen, two other things caught my eye. One was a colorful needlepoint fastened to the inside of the casket lid, with the words *Idle Hands Are the Devil's Playground* neatly stitched onto the canvas. I remembered seeing a print hanging on Grandma's kitchen wall above the refrigerator with the exact same words.

The second thing I found fascinating was a highly polished

spread of food. I knew my grandma made one of the desserts—a quince pie.

I spotted the boy who had been sitting in front of us in church. He was holding hands with some girl with long golden curls. Crap!

So I ate and drank and ate some more until Grandma said it was time to go home.

*****

"That's the same as the needlepoint in Diggy's casket," I said, looking at the print on the kitchen wall. Grandma and I were sitting at the table drinking tea. We'd just returned from the funeral. "What does it mean?"

Grandma glanced up at the print.

"Ah, the Devil's Playground," she said, nodding. "You know, I was an orphan, pretty much grew up over at St. Angeles."

I nodded. My father had told me the story.

"Got to admit," said Grandma, looking somewhat sheepish, "I warn't the best girl while I was there. Used to get into a lot of trouble. Got my knuckles rapped more'n once by old Sister Abigail. Truth be told, I was pretty headstrong. Didn't want to do nothin' I was told. Guess I was resentful my ma and pa both up and died on me and left me an orphan.

"Anyways, one day, I guess I was about your age, Sister gail, she takes me by the hand and marches me down to the en where some woman was cookin' for the evenin' meal. y,' she says to her, 'this is Miss Rebecca Overmeyer. do somethin' with her.'

en the old sister, she turns around and leaves. And m, standin' there lookin' at this little old lady—okay, I ybe she warn't so old then, just looked old to me—

164

wooden rolling pin cradled in Diggy McNamara's right arm.

Mrs. McNamara did not appear to be a large woman, except for her hands, which I thought to be enormous. I figured that was the reason the rolling pin, while of normal size, had really, *really* big handles.

We stood there a long time without saying anything. Then Grandma began to softly cry. She reached into her dress sleeve, removed a lace handkerchief, and gingerly dabbed her eyes.

She took my hand again and led me to a pew about halfway back down the aisle, where we sat down and were soon joined by the other women Grandma had been with in the narthex. I wanted to ask her about the rolling pin but she put her finger to her mouth, indicating I should be still.

Brother Young's eulogy was, how best to say this? Long. To tell the truth I didn't pay much attention. I was far too busy looking around at all the people gathered there. The place was so crowded many of them stood lined up along the back wall and down the sides of the room. I took particular interest in one boy about my age a few pews ahead of us and wondered how difficult it would be to strike up a conversation with b when this was all over and done with.

I did catch a few words the minister said, like *qui orphanage*. When he mentioned *rolling pin* I started attention but apparently he had already said everythi going to say about that subject.

The cemetery was right across the road from everybody walked over there after the service. more attention to what Brother Young said more about that rolling pin. But all he tall like *ashes to ashes* and *dust to dust*.

Following the graveside service, e across the road and downstairs to th the ladies of the Baptist Mission holdin' a rollin' pin in her hand and me wonderin' what in the world it was she was goin' to "do" with me. Beat me with that rollin' pin? Make me scrub floors? I didn't know. At that moment I sure warn't feelin' too headstrong.

"Diggy stared at me for a moment, then said, *'Grab that apron behind you and put it on.'*

"Her voice was real calm and reassurin' and I commenced to feelin' a tad better. While I was puttin' the apron on, I noticed the needlepoint on the wall."

*What's that mean? I asked*

*'Why'd you put the snake in Sister Justine's bed?'*

"I tell you, my mouth dropped open. How'd she know? I hadn't confessed to anyone what I'd done, except my best friend, Gracie. I was purty sure even Sister Abigail hadn't found out about it, since I hadn't been punished."

*'How'd you know 'bout that?' I asked.*

*'Ain't much goes on 'round here I don't know 'bout,' she answered. 'I even know stuff Sister Abigail don't. So, how come?'*

I looked down at the floor, embarrassed I'd been found out. *'I was bored,'* I said. *'Just wanted to shake things up a little.'*

Diggy chuckled. *'You sure did that. 'Course, poor old Sister durn near had a heart attack when she pulled back the sheet, and there the thing was, starin' up at her.'*

"And that was all she said about that. At the time I didn't understand what my puttin' a snake in Sister Justine's bed had to do with the devil and his playground, but later on, I got the message.

"Diggy was head cook at the orphanage; had been since 'fore I got there. That day was the start of my learnin' time under Diggy McNamara. Over the next six years, until I turned eighteen and left St. Angeles, she taught me what my ma would have if she had lived, like how to sew and crochet and do needlepoint and cook. But what I loved best was the bakin'.

We'd bake bread and cookies and muffins and pies—everythin' you could think of."

"How about the rolling pin?" I asked, "The one in the casket?."

"Ah, the rollin' pin. That was a gift to Diggy."

"A gift?"

Grandma took a sip of tea. "It was about ten years ago," she said. "One evenin' Diggy was there later than usual, bakin' pies for the next day, which was a holiday of some sort. She heard a commotion outside the door and when she went out she saw one of the orphanage girls and a man she didn't know. He was tryin' to force himself on the girl, and she was tryin' to fight him off. Diggy took one look and conked the man right on the head with her rollin' pin. Hit him so hard she cracked his skull; knocked him out cold. Also cracked her rollin' pin.

"Somebody called the sheriff and when he got there the man was still unconscious. Seemed he'd only just got into town and was wanted by the police up in Cincinnati, where he'd raped four or five girls."

"Was that the rolling pin in the coffin?" I asked.

"Nope," said Grandma. "That was a special pin there in the casket."

"Special how?"

"After Diggy cracked her rollin' pin, me and some of the girls, the ones who 'grew up' in Diggy's kitchen—I warn't the only one, we got kind of a 'club,' you know—we got together and got Mr. Jessup to make her a new one on his lathe, with extra big handles. Most pins are made out of maple, but this one was made out of coffeetree. It was Diggy's pride and joy and that's why we put it in the casket with her, God rest her soul."

Grandma's eyes misted over.

"She sounds like a nice woman," I said.

"Nice don't begin to cover it," replied Grandma. "Diggy McNamara was, without a doubt, a saint. Like I said, she taught me everythin' I know about cookin' and bakin'. Not just me, neither. Lots of women in this town who grew up at St. Angeles owe whatever cookin' skills they have to Diggy. She taught me a lot more, too."

"How's that?"

"I told you I was a pretty headstrong girl. Truth is, I didn't think much of myself. I'd been at St. Angeles over seven years by the time I met Diggy, and by then I knew I was never goin' to get adopted. I figured it was because I was such a loser.

"About a week after I showed up in her kitchen Diggy brought in some real ugly things that looked like grapefruits, except they had spines all over them."

"Quinces!" I said.

"Yep, quinces. I'd seen them out on the tree in the back yard at the orphanage but I didn't know what they was. They looked terrible and they smelled worse.

*'We're goin' to make some quince pies,'* Diggy said.

I wrinkled up my nose. *'What'll it taste like?'* I asked.

Diggy smiled. *'You'll see.'*

"First, we made the dough and put it in the 'frigerator to chill a bit. Then she showed me how to peel the quince and told me to take a bite. Lawd, it was terrible! Worse than the look and the smell. I almost throwed up.

*'Pretty bad, huh?'* said Diggy.

"I could only nod. I couldn't even speak, I had such a bad taste in my mouth.

*'Wait 'til you see what we can do with this,'* said Diggy.

"Throw it out was my bet.

But, no, she showed me how to core and grate it, then do the same to the second quince.

*'Quince got to be grated, not sliced,'* said Diggy. *"Cause if you do*

167

*'em in chunks they take too long to cook.'*

"She showed me how to peel and core and slice the apples, over two pounds of them. I thought I'd never finish.

"But I did. Then Diggy showed me how to mix everythin' together with sugar and water.

"By this time the dough was ready to roll out. Diggy had me scatter some flour on the big cuttin' board, then handed me the rollin' pin and showed me how to roll out the crusts, always rollin' the dough away from me, turnin' as I went, and keepin' the rollin' pin and the board floured to keep the dough from stickin'.

"When I finished we placed the crusts in the pie pans, spooned in the fillin', and popped 'em in the oven. Diggy fixed us some tea and we sat down to wait for the pies to bake.

"While we was sittin' there, Diggy asked me if I ever thought about how much a pie is kind of like life.

"Now, that didn't make no sense to me at all, but I didn't say nothin'.

*'Think about it,'* she said. *'To make the dough you take things like flour and salt and sugar and water and cut 'em all in wit a dough fork. All kinds of things go into makin' us what we are, and when the cuttin's goin' on sometimes it feels like we're bein' pulled ever which way. Then when the dough's ready, you roll it out into the crust. Didn't you ever feel like life was rollin' right over you?'*

"Boy, that was for sure!

*'Then you take the fillin', like these here quinces. Now, let's be honest, them quinces don't look or smell all that good, but we peel 'em and grate 'em and plop 'em in the crust, stick 'em in a oven until they're baked and come out smellin' and tastin' delicious. People's like that too, I reckon. You look at some and they don't seem like much on the outside. But a little bakin' and they turn out to be purty good after all. Yep, I think pies are pretty much like people and their lives.'*

"I might not have understood the point earlier she was

168

tryin' to make about the snake in Sister Justine's bed and the Devil's Playground, but somehow I knew now she was talkin' 'bout me. From that moment on I began to feel good about myself, 'cause I knew I was goin' to taste good.

"And that's how I learned to bake quince pies."

One question remained.

"So," I asked, "how did Diggy get her name?"

Grandma shrugged. "Don't know. I never asked and she never told me. Now, go grab that there apron off the doorknob and put it on."

"How come?" I asked, glancing at the apron.

"'Cause I'm goin' to teach you how to make a quince pie," said Grandma.

## MORCHELLAS
1977

It thought it could hide from me, but it could not.

Even after twenty years I could still spot a morel or, as mycologists like to call them, a *Morchella*.

This one peeked out at me from its hiding place, its cream-colored head trying its best to blend in with the leaves that partly covered it. But there was no mistaking that shape, that texture, that so closely resembles a piece of Swiss cheese, or an ocean or sea sponge, an appearance that sometimes causes these delicacies of nature to be called "sponge" mushrooms.

I'd been a "shroomer" since I was a kid, going out first with my father, later with him and my older brother, Merle. It was an annual springtime ritual: April came, we went mushroom hunting.

Then I joined the Navy and for the last twenty years was stationed in places where morels didn't grow; exotic places such as Spain and Cuba and Hawaii, places where the word *mushroom* to a local meant, if anything, something small and white and round that you find in the supermarket in a can. I suppose other mushrooms might have grown in those places but I was a purist—nothing short of true morels counted as "authentic" eating mushrooms.

Now, having recently retired, I was back home in Chickapea County, Kentucky. And for the first time, since I left there in 1957, I was hunting mushrooms.

I stood for a few minutes, looking around, checking out my surroundings. The mushroom would wait—it wasn't going anywhere. It's always a good idea, you see, to notice in what kind of terrain you're finding morels, although, as my dad always told us boys, "Son, you can find mushrooms anywhere, but you can't find them everywhere."

The landscape around me here was different from any I'd ever hunted before: a newly cleared fairway for a golf course for the Chickapea Country Club, a golf course that was never built, due to a lack of funds.

Moderately dense woods lined the sides of the fairway, which was about fifty yards wide. Although almost all the trees had been cut down, their stumps, dozens of them, still stood as silent testimonies to what they had once been. The fairway was covered with small patches of grass, weeds, and plants with long fuzzy leaves that could pass for rabbit's ears—if the rabbit were green, along with the previous winter's leaves that the trees bordering either side of the clearing had reluctantly allowed to escape their branches. It was all ground cover that spread a patchwork quilt over the earth that formed the base of it all, still damp from the morning rain. Here and there I saw lonely sentinels, smaller trees that had not, for some reason, been leveled with the others.

And the smell! It even *smelled* like mushrooms, that pungent, somewhat musty odor of decaying wood and leaves. For a few moments, I closed my eyes and breathed in the heavenly aroma.

But then—it was time to pick.

Carefully making my way to where the mushroom crouched, I was careful where I stepped, ensuring I didn't trample others that were more successful in concealing their whereabouts.

There was one! And another! My, God—a half dozen or more growing in a clump!

Excitedly—and, a bit nervous, I must admit—I knelt down and, grasping a morel at the base of its stem, broke it off, wishing I'd remembered to bring a knife with me. It was about half again as large as my fist, and a good five inches in height. The others were all about the same size.

I allowed my gaze to wander a little farther and spotted more little cream-colored "sponges," some obvious, others attempting, as had the first one, to escape detection, doing their best to conceal themselves behind, or under, some cover.

Five hours later, tired from kneeling down and bending over, sweat pouring down my face, my neck, my back, my arms, the hot sun beating down, and with my mesh bag full of morels, I made my way back to the car. I felt terrific!

Tomorrow I'd come back and look some more. And I'd get Merle to come with me.

After all, there were still seventeen more fairways to go.

## ANGELS IN THE CHRISTMAS TREE
## 1986

I'd almost forgotten the glasses.

But there they were, tucked inside an envelope, hidden under a flap of the cardboard box that held our Christmas tree ornaments.

Ten years. It had been ten years since I'd last seen those glasses.

They weren't real glasses. They were special 3-D glasses, a pair Jennie got on our trip to Disneyland in 1986. It was her tenth birthday, November 30th, and the 3-D movie, Captain Eo, starring Michael Jackson, had been playing there for a little over two months.

Funny how things—events, objects, experiences, relationships—which seemed so significant at the time recede into our memory. Until they bubble back up to the surface of our consciousness. Like these glasses. And then, once again, we're reminded of how important they truly were.

I put the glasses on and walked into the living room, where Linda and I had minutes before finished stringing lights on the Christmas tree.

There they were! Just like ten years ago!

I felt my chest tighten, and my eyes begin to tear as the memories of that period of our life washed over me in a wave.

1986. The year that changed our lives forever.

∞

It started innocently enough one morning when Linda and I awoke to find Jennie at the foot of our bed, crying.

"Honey, what is it? What's wrong?" I asked.

"My head hurts, Daddy."

"Did you hit it on something?"

"No," said Jennie, sniffling. "It was hurting when I woke up."

"I'll get you some aspirin," said Linda, springing up from the bed.

"Come up here with me until Mommy gets back," I said, extending my arms.

Jennie crawled up onto the bed and slid under the blanket, next to me.

"It really hurts, Daddy."

"I know it does, honey. Mommy will be right back, and you'll feel better real soon."

By noon Jennie felt well enough to go to the Memorial Day parade with us. We didn't think any more about it.

About two weeks later, it happened again.

Jennie woke up with a terrible headache. This time aspirin did little to assuage the pain. Within hours she was vomiting, violent eruptions that wracked her tiny body. It was time to get her to a doctor.

\*\*\*\*\*

"I think I know what Jennie's problem is."

It was apparent from the expression on the doctor's face the news wasn't good.

"On a hunch, I had Jennie's eyes examined. She doesn't wear glasses, does she?"

"No," said Linda. "She's always had perfect vision."

"We detected some weakness in her right eye. That, and the headaches and the vomiting lead me to suspect she may have a brain tumor."

Linda's hands went immediately to her mouth. I stared ahead, blankly. Neither of us spoke for what seemed forever.

When I recovered my senses enough I asked, "Are you sure?"

"No," said the doctor. "The only way we can know for sure is to do surgery, go in and see what we find."

"Is that dangerous?" asked Linda.

"It can be," said the doctor. "But, as I said, it's the only way we can know for sure. And I think the symptoms are evident enough to warrant the risk."

"And what if you do find a tumor?" I asked.

"We would remove it."

"And she'd be okay?"

The doctor hesitated for a moment before answering. "Depends. On how big the tumor is, and how extensive it might be."

"When would you do it?" asked Linda.

"We'd want to take her to Louisville, to U. of L. The hospital there has an outstanding neurosurgery department. I've already spoken with them, and they can schedule the operation for the day after tomorrow."

"It should be done right away then, you think?"

The concern on Linda's face was evident as she spoke.

"I do. If it's a fast growing tumor, the sooner we can get it out the better Jennie's chances of a full recovery."

"All right," I said. "Let's do it."

"I'll take care of all the arrangements," said the doctor.

175

"You need to have Jennie at the hospital by noon tomorrow, so she can be admitted, and the proper preparations made."

None of us spoke on the way home. I could tell Jennie was concerned about the examination she'd undergone, but she said nothing.

Later that evening, after supper, we told her she'd be going into the hospital the next day for some more tests. We didn't mention the tumor.

It wasn't until after Jennie went to bed that Linda broke down. Huge tears rolled down her cheeks, and her whole upper body shook violently. I held her in my arms, doing my best to reassure her with my presence and with my words that everything would be fine. But I wasn't all that sure myself.

We left early the next morning for Louisville. By ten o'clock Jennie was admitted and in her room. I went to find a motel for us for the night, while Linda stayed with Jennie.

*****

I don't know how long the surgery took, but it seemed like days.

When the surgeon finally came into the waiting room to speak with Linda and me, I knew at once all was not right.

"It is definitely a tumor," he said. "We were able to remove perhaps a quarter of it, but the rest is so wrapped around the brain it was impossible to get it all."

"What does that mean?" I managed to get out.

"We'll set up a program of chemotherapy and try to destroy the rest of it that way." The doctor hesitated a moment before continuing. "But, I have to be honest with you; it doesn't look good."

Linda began to weep, but unlike the night before, this time softly, almost to herself.

"I'm sorry," said the doctor.

"Yes, thank you," I replied, not sure what else I should say.

By the time Jennie started school that fall, most of her hair had fallen out. She had always been somewhat thin, but now it was apparent she was rapidly getting even thinner.

At the four-month checkup in October, we got the bad news.

"It's not working," said the doctor, shaking his head. "The chemotherapy's not working."

"What does that mean?" asked Linda in a faltering voice.

"Three months, six at the most. It's time you start preparing for the inevitable."

"She's dying?" I asked, incredulously.

The doctor nodded. "Yes. I'm so sorry."

When we broke the news to Jennie, she cried for a few moments. Then she wiped the tears from her eyes and said, "I guess it means I'll get to see Grandma and Grandpa all that much sooner."

That's when both Linda and I lost it. We started bawling.

Jennie came over and put her arms around both of us. "Don't cry," she said. "I'll be all right."

*****

"What would you like to do for your birthday?"

Jennie looked up at me from her bowl of cereal. "Anything?" she asked.

I laughed. "Within reason."

"I'd like to go to Disneyland one last time."

My heart caught in my throat. *One last time.*

"Okay," I said. "Disneyland it is."

And that's where Jennie got the glasses.

When she found out Michael Jackson's movie was playing

177

there, her spirits soared. "He is *so* cool!" she said. *Captain Eo* was the first place we went after going through the gates.

I'll have to admit, it *was* pretty cool.

I'd seen 3-D movies before, but when those *things*—were they bats? I don't remember now—came flying at me, I ducked!

Jennie went back in two more times that day to see the movie. Linda and I welcomed the opportunity to rest our feet.

Both Linda and Jennie slept on the ride back to the motel. Once, when I glanced at the rear-view mirror to see if Jennie was still asleep, I saw the glasses clasped firmly in her hands.

*****

I looked forward to Christmas that year with mixed emotions. I knew it would be Jennie's last one. For that, I was sad. But I was also extremely grateful that at least we'd have *this* one.

Two weeks before Christmas I put up the Christmas tree and strung the lights. Linda and Jennie spent the next hour or so putting on the ornaments.

Later that evening, Linda and I were sitting in the living room, reading, when Jennie came in wearing her 3-D glasses.

"Did you know we've got angels in our Christmas tree?" she asked.

"Sure," said Linda. "As I recall, there are four or five. There's the one Aunt . . ."

"No, no," Jennie interrupted. "I mean, they're all over the tree. Hundreds of them. I can see them with my glasses."

Not one to pass up seeing hundreds of angels—and in my Christmas tree to boot—I said, "Let me have your glasses. I want to see them."

Jennie handed me the glasses and I put them on. She led us

178

into the family room, where the tree stood.

Jennie was right!

Through the glasses, every light on the tree took the form of an angel!

Outlined in red with green shading—Christmas colors, naturally!—were angels, each sporting two distinct wings. Crowns adorned their heads, and they held long trumpets to their mouths as if to herald the coming of the King.

"Let me see," said Linda.

"Oh, my God," she exclaimed, putting on the glasses. "They're so beautiful!"

"Hey, hey," said Jennie. "They're *my* angels. I found them. Can I have my glasses back, please?"

Linda grinned and handed the glasses to Jennie, who immediately placed them back on her nose. I took Linda's hand, and we smiled at each other. It was the happiest we had seen our daughter in weeks.

On Christmas Eve we decided to go to church. Neither Linda nor I had ever been particularly religious, to the point where unlike most "C and E" Christians—Christmas and Easter—we didn't even go on those holidays. In fact, as nearly as we could remember, the last time we were in church was when Jennie was baptized, and only then because Linda's parents insisted on it.

But this Christmas was different. It would be Jennie's last.

I don't remember what the sermon was about. I *do* remember singing the hymns, though, words that in recent years I'd only heard from choirs at the mall, or on television. Jennie sat between Linda and me, and for much of the service we all held each other's hands.

After we arrived back home, Linda and I were in the kitchen enjoying hot eggnogs. Jennie was engaged in what now was her favorite pastime: watching the angels in the Christmas tree.

Suddenly, she burst into the kitchen, her face flushed, waving the glasses in one hand.

"An angel!" she cried. "I saw an angel!"

"Whoa, settle down," I said. "You mean you saw a couple of hundred angels, don't you?"

"No, no, you don't understand," said Jennie, obviously excited. "I was looking at the angels in the tree when all of a sudden one of them came down from the branches and floated right over to me. It hung in the air there in front of me, and then it took the horn away from its mouth, and I saw the horn had changed into a big sword. Then the angel took the sword and touched me on the head—you know, like when somebody gets knighted? And then she spoke to me!"

"It was a girl angel?" I said.

"Uh, huh."

"And the angel spoke to you?" asked Linda. "What did she say?"

"She said, 'All is well.'"

"All is well? Is that all she said?" I asked.

"Yes," said Jennie.

"What do you think that means?" asked Linda.

"I think it means . . ."

∞

The sound of the doorbell brought me back to the present.

"Sweetheart," Linda called from the kitchen, where she was preparing dinner. "Would you see if that's the kids?"

Still holding the glasses in my hand, I walked over to the door and peered through the glass pane at the top. There, standing in the snow, holding my new granddaughter, Angel, in his arms, was my son-in-law, Brad, and next to him my

180

beautiful, fully healed, wonderful twenty-year-old daughter, Jennie.

*Yes, all is well*, I thought. All is well!

# THE POOL BOY
## 1989

Growing up in St. Cloud, Minnesota and freezing my ass off every winter—which ran from mid-September through the end of May—I vowed when I was old enough I would move south, where it was warm all the time . . . or so I thought.

So, when I was twenty-one, I did move south—all the way to Minneapolis, some seventy-two miles away! All right, it wasn't Florida or Arizona. Hell, it wasn't even Texas. But it was a start in the right direction.

When I was twenty-two I met Harry.

He was from southern California originally. And why anyone would leave southern California to come to Minnesota was beyond me. But his company had transferred him there, and he had a very good job. Good enough that when we got married I quit my job at the water company and became a full-time housewife—and within ten months a full-time mother.

Two more kids and ten years later, Harry was with another company, in an even better job. The day he came home and told me the company was transferring him to their plant in Kentucky I got down on my knees and gave thanks to God! A warm climate at last! Okay, so I found out that, while it's warmer than Minnesota, Kentucky can still get pretty damn cold at times.

Now, here I am, a forty-seven-year-old woman living in Camptown—by myself.

Oh, yes, Harry went through his mid-life crisis, and in the process found another twenty-two-year-old "chickie" to marry. God, was *I* ever that young? That immature? That *stupid?* All our kids were grown and gone, one back to Minnesota, one to New York, and the other overseas in the military.

But I can't kick. By the time the divorce rolled around Harry had climbed the corporate ladder to where he was pulling down over six figures a year. *Well* over.

As a result, we owned this gorgeous four-bedroom, million-dollar home in the most exclusive area of Camptown, a gated community adjacent to the Chickapea Country Club with the pretentious name of *Paradise Village,* which I got in the divorce settlement, along with a monthly alimony payment from Harry of fifteen hundred dollars. Plus the Lexus. And the bonds. And stocks. And about everything else poor Harry and I owned.

Okay, I let him keep the Volvo.

Now he and his new wife—Mindy or Mandy, something like that—live in a condo a few miles away in Crownsville. I've seen the place. It's okay.

But it sure ain't Paradise Village!

Today is not one of those cold days I mentioned. In fact, it's about a hundred and forty in the shade, and I'm relaxing in a chaise lounge on the deck that surrounds the in-ground swimming pool. Most all the houses in our little community have in-ground pools. Hell, I didn't know there *was* such a creature as an outdoor, in-ground swimming pool before I came to Kentucky!

By the way, Harry's condo has a teeny, tiny, pool that serves all twenty-seven units.

I could go inside where it's air-conditioned. But, no, here I am in my bikini in my chaise lounge, a cold glass of rum and coke pressed against my forehead, lathered up with sunscreen, and trying to come up with something to write. Oh, and did I mention? I finally convinced the features editor of the local paper, the *Camptown Southern Gazette*, to give me a try at writing an article. Not that I need a job; or the money. It's just so damn *boring* doing nothing.

I can't exactly say I'm thrilled with the topic she gave me, though: how men and women approach sex differently.

Let's face it: men want sex, women want sex—what's the difference? Unfortunately, I haven't gotten any lately. Not that I couldn't, if I really wanted to. I mean, even at forty-seven I'm still a pretty good-looking woman—five-nine, one-hundred and thirty-two pounds; thirty-six, twenty-five, thirty-seven. Naturally blonde hair. You know what I'm talking about. Let's face it—I've still got it. It's just that, after what Harry did to me, I have a little trouble trusting men. But, hey, I guess you don't have to trust them to have sex with them, do you? Except to make sure they're wearing some protection, so you don't get AIDS or one of those other sexually transmitted diseases.

Wait! Maybe that's the angle I need! *I* can get sex anytime I want it. All I'd have to do is walk up to some guy and say, "You wanna fuck?" and off we'd go. But if a man tried that he'd probably get slapped or thrown in jail.

"Mrs. Martin?"

I look up, startled. I hadn't heard anybody come around the side of the house.

Then I see who it is: Eddie, the pool boy. He comes on Thursdays to clean and service the pool.

"Oh, hi, Eddie. I didn't hear you coming."

"You looked like you were deep in thought."

"Yeah, I was." I can tell Eddie's trying hard not to be too obvious in checking me out. Poor kid. It's a little difficult since

184

I'm sprawled out on the chaise, with no more than two percent of my body covered.

"You're here to do the pool."

"Huh? Oh—oh, yes," he stammers. "I mean, if that's all right. If you're planning on using it right now, I can come back later."

"No, now's fine."

He turns away from me and starts for the shed where we keep the pool equipment. Now it's *my* turn to check *Eddie* out. Not as if I haven't before. But thinking about the topic of my article is giving me a whole new perspective on this young man.

I say "young" because he can't be more than about twenty-five—about the same age as my oldest, Sam. Tall, with a terrific tan, incredibly intense brown eyes, and endowed with that seemingly natural muscular build these mountain men have when they're young—before the beer and the fried chicken and too much other Crisco food turns them into potbellied, middle-aged lumps.

What I appreciate most about Eddie, though, is his ass: he has a really nice, tight ass! And the form-fitting short shorts he's wearing serve marvelously as an enhancement to the obvious.

Oh, well, quit drooling and get back to work.

Men and women and sex. I start writing, and for the next fifteen minutes get pretty far into the premise of my article: that even if men *do* want sex more than women—and I'm pretty damn sure they do—it's easier for women to get it. I'm about to jot down a few examples when I look up and notice Eddie has removed his tee-shirt. Like my body, his, too, is drenched with perspiration, which causes tiny diamonds to dance all over the muscles of his back. But the moisture I'm feeling now between my legs, under my bikini thong is definitely *not* sweat.

So I take off my bikini top.

Hell, I mean, if Eddie can take off his tee-shirt, why can't I take off my bikini top? After all, this is *my* backyard! And with a seven-foot-high wooden fence around the whole pool area, there's no danger of any neighbors seeing me. Not that I give a rat's ass if they did.

With a great deal of reluctance, I take my eyes off Eddie and start to write.

*As Felicity rose sensually from her chaise lounge, she noticed Eduardo, her pool boy, had taken off his tee-shirt. His muscles tensed as he moved his long hose around the pool's bottom, sucking up the debris. Quietly, she removed her bathing suit, sneaked up behind him, and pinched his butt. He turned to see her standing there, naked, all two hundred and twenty pounds of her. She grinned, showing a gap where three of her front teeth used to be. "Would you like to fuck me?" she asked. Without a word, Eduardo slipped out of his trunks and started to pick Felicity up in his muscular arms to carry her back to the chaise lounge. Then he thought better of it, took her hand, and instead led her to the lounge, where the two of them made mad, passionate love for the next hour.*

Now for the other side.

*Harry took a long slug from his bourbon and water and gazed longingly at Chastity, the new pool girl he'd just hired. At thirty-five, he was in the prime of his life and still possessed the terrific build he'd acquired playing football and wrestling, in high school and college. He was single and rich. And more than one woman told him he looked a lot like Antonio Banderas.*

*He guessed Chastity to be in her mid-twenties. At about five-foot-three and less than one hundred pounds, her figure left a lot to be desired. The straw-colored hair framed a sort of cute face that had at one time done battle with a bad case of acne—and lost. But Harry was horny.*

*He sauntered over to Chastity and gently tapped her on the shoulder. She looked around, startled.*

*"Chastity, I'd like to ask you something," said Harry. "I couldn't help but notice how attractive you are, and I was wondering how you'd feel about taking a break to join me upstairs in my bedroom for some wine and a little fooling around."*

*Harry wasn't at all prepared for the slap that almost tore his head off. He was, however, prepared and waiting with his attorney for the police officers who arrived about a half-hour later, as he'd heard Chastity as she stormed away yelling words like "sex maniac," and "rape," and "I'm calling the cops."*

I lay my pencil down. So, I wonder, is this how it would play out in the majority of cases? The woman, no matter if she weren't a raving beauty, only had to issue the invitation in order to get laid? And the man, even a gorgeous, single, rich guy, would not only get rejected but maybe get sued or go to jail?

Or was my theory full of holes?

Out of the corner of my eye, I can see Eddie watching me out of the corner of *his* eye. I wonder how long he's been ogling me.

I lay down the yellow legal pad on which I've been writing, get up and walk over to where Eddie is bent over, working on something. Finally, when I'm standing right in front of him, he stops what he's doing and straightens up. He has trouble keeping his eyes off my breasts. I reach out and raise his chin so he's now looking directly into my eyes.

"Eddie," I say, loosening the ties on my bikini thong, allowing it to fall to the deck, "I'm doing a little survey, and I need your participation."

Best damn survey I ever participated in!

## THE EMPTY CLOSET
## 1992

". . . the next mayor of Camptown, Kentucky—Richard Townsend!"

Richard made his way to the podium as the three thousand people packed into the Camptown High School Auditorium rose to their feet and gave him a thunderous ovation.

He waited for the applause to die down, his gaze taking in the crowd that had come to support him in his campaign. Many he knew personally; others were complete strangers to him, although not he to them. He waited and waved his hands—but his mind was somewhere else. His thoughts were of David, and how much had changed between the two of them in the short month just past.

Had it been only four weeks ago that David brought the subject up?

*****

"Richard, I want to come out."

"What do you mean, 'come out'?"

"I mean I want to tell people I'm gay."

"Are you fucking crazy? Why the hell would you want to do that? And why now, with the election less than two months

188

away?"

David looked at Richard, the pain evident in his eyes.

"You know why now."

He knew. David was dying. After five years of living with AIDS, he could fight it off no longer. The damn disease had caught up with him.

"But why come out at all?" Richard asked, a softer tone to his voice now. "Why would you want everyone to know: your parents, your brother, the people in your office, your former teammates? What would that accomplish?"

"Because I'm tired of living a lie. I'm tired of not admitting what I am, of *who* I am. I'm not ashamed of being gay. What I *am* ashamed of is not having the courage to admit it to the world."

For a while, neither of them spoke. Then, Richard broke the silence.

"You know, this would wreck my chances of being elected."

David looked at him in surprise. "Why?"

"Why? You have to ask *why*? How many people do you think will vote for me when they find out I'm gay? For God's sake, this is *Camptown*, not San Francisco!"

"But . . . how would they find out? No one knows about us."

Richard gave him a withering look that said *how naive can you be?*

"Shit, David, people are going to put two and two together. It's no secret we're good friends. We go out drinking together, we go to sporting events together. We take trips together. The only thing we *don't* do is double date. I imagine people already have their suspicions. Your coming out would just confirm it for them. I'd be plastered all over the front page of the *Gazette*."

189

"Richard, I'd never do anything to hurt you."

"This would."

"Let's drop it for now, okay."

"Fine."

Over the next several weeks they didn't talk any more about David's desire to go public. But every day Richard watched him become more withdrawn. The life, the spirit, seemed to drain away, little by little. He knew much of it could be attributed to David's rapidly failing physical condition. But it was more than that. No matter how bad things got in the past—and there were times when they had gotten especially bad—David always remained upbeat, positive, evidencing a spark, a thirst for life, that Richard doubted he, himself, could sustain under similar circumstances. But now. . .

\*\*\*\*\*

"David, what's wrong?"

David looked up from the book he was reading: *Coming Out: An Act of Love*, by Rob Eichberg.

"You mean besides the obvious fact I'm dying?" he said. For a brief moment, he allowed a smile to cross his lips.

Richard put down the glass of wine he'd been holding and knelt in front of David.

"Yes, besides that. Something else is going on."

"You know what," said David.

"Your wanting to come out?"

David nodded.

"I don't know why it's so important to you," said Richard.

"Because, as I told you, I'm tired of living a lie . . . and because I love you."

Richard stared at him. He didn't understand.

"We've been together five years," said David. "We've been

lovers all that time. But we don't live together because people might 'suspect.' Richard, I'm proud of our relationship. I *want* people to know how I feel about you. Okay, I realize that's not possible because you have an image to maintain. But, if I came out, in a way that would say for me—*to* me—that *I*, at least, acknowledge what we mean to each other. I know you can't understand that, that it doesn't make any sense to you. But that's how I feel."

Richard shook his head and stood.

"You're right," he said. "I don't understand."

"I know," said David. He went back to reading his book.

The next day he was admitted to the hospital.

Every minute Richard could spare away from his office, he was at David's side. The pain killers David received kept him groggy much of the time, but from time to time he would awaken and find Richard there. On those rare occasions they talked—of the good times they'd spent together, especially the traveling: the trip to Scotland, where Richard had always wanted to go; the trip to Disneyland where *David* had always wanted to go!; the two weeks spent by themselves alone in the Great Smoky Mountains one summer, in a cabin outside Gatlinburg, waking up each morning and walking out onto the front porch, naked to the world, standing with their arms around each another, gazing in wonder at the shroud of mist that covered the landscape like a mantle of fine linen cloth. Then they had gone back inside, into the bedroom, and made love.

Every day.

It all seemed so long ago.

The night before his televised rally, Richard stayed late at the hospital, past normal visiting hours. The nurses looked the other way. David slept most of the time, so Richard sat and held his hand. He was about to leave when David woke up.

"Hi," said Richard.

"Hi, yourself," said David, his voice no more than a whisper.

"I have to go now, but I'll stop by in the morning before I go to the office. I've given a lot of thought to what you want to do. Let's talk about it then."

"Okay." David managed a weak grin.

Richard bent over and kissed him.

"Goodnight."

"Goodnight." David mouthed the words, "I love you."

*****

"Ladies and gentlemen, City Councilman and the next mayor of our fair city—Richard Townsend!"

"Friends, coworkers," said Richard, "for the last nine months, we have worked side by side on this campaign. During that time I've looked forward with confidence, due to your unflagging efforts, to winning this race, and serving as your mayor."

Another round of applause.

"I still have hopes it might happen."

A stillness descended over the auditorium.

"This morning, as many of you know, our community lost a great citizen: David Jeffers."

Out of the corner of his eye, Richard saw Alex, his campaign manager, frantically flipping the pages of the script, then staring at Richard as if to say, "What the hell are you doing?"

Richard ignored him.

"David Jeffers was not only a great athlete, an All-American at the University of Kentucky, and an All-Pro cornerback in the National Football League for seven seasons, he was also

192

one of the finest attorneys this city has ever known; a close, personal friend of mine; and undoubtedly the most courageous person I've ever known. But there was more to David Jeffers than just those things." Richard hesitated, then added, "He was also gay."

A murmur ran through the crowd.

"I can say this without betraying any confidences because David wanted to go public with his sexual orientation before he died. He was tired of living a lie. The reason he didn't go public . . . was because I wouldn't let him." The auditorium was absolutely still, except for an occasional cough, and the shuffling of feet.

"The reason I wouldn't let him say anything was because I was afraid it would hurt my chances of winning this election. You see, for the last five years, David and I have been lovers. Like him, I, too, am gay. I finally realized he was right. I've been living the same lie he was living, afraid to admit my sexuality, reluctant to acknowledge what, and who, I really am. Now you know. For the record: I loved David Jeffers. I still do. I always will."

Richard walked back to his seat and sat down. He felt as if a huge weight was lifted from him. Whatever happened from here on out, he knew, it would be okay.

More importantly, he knew David would have been proud of him.

## NICE GUYS . . .
## 1996

I remember the first time I met Jack.

A rawboned, just-out-of-high-school catcher from some backwater town named Nowata, located somewhere in the northeast corner of Oklahoma, he might as well have worn a big sign around his neck reading "Okie."

He was cute, he was well built, he was shy, he was almost unbelievably polite—*nice* is the word that comes to mind—and, although I didn't find this out until years later, he was smart, too. Plus, he was a helluva ballplayer, even if he *was* only eighteen years old. At least, that's the impression I got from what was being said around the front office.

Everybody—everybody who was *anybody*, that is—said he was going to be the next Mickey Mantle or Johnny Bench, two other fellows from Oklahoma who—I found out later—had been pretty good players. Johnny had retired the previous year, I was told, and since he and Jack were both catchers, the comparison of the two was natural.

The year was 1984. At the time, I was a clerk in the front office of the Louisville Redbirds, the Triple-A farm club of the St. Louis Cardinals. I was pretty new myself, having been on the job for about a month, following my graduation from Indiana University. To say I knew nothing about baseball would be an understatement. The first time I heard a player stole second base I thought he'd end up in jail, or at least be fined by the judge. Sociology was my major at I.U., and the only sport I was familiar with was track and field. And that was because my boyfriend at the time was a shot-putter. When he first told me what he did, I thought shot-putting had something to do with drinking whiskey.

But there I was, at the age of twenty-two, working for a professional baseball team, thanks to my uncle Marvin, who happened to be a groundskeeper at the stadium. He'd heard about this job opening, and knew I was about to graduate, figured I probably couldn't get a job "doing sociology," as he put it, and talked the personnel manager into giving me the job—even before he'd asked me if I wanted it. When he told me about it, I told him thanks, but I didn't think professional baseball was in my career path, and I could put my sociology degree to work for me when I graduated, thank you very much.

I sure was glad he talked the personnel manager into holding the position for me.

After two months of discovering out how much—how little—a degree in sociology was worth, I was happy to be hired by the Louisville Redbirds Professional Baseball Team.

But, back to Jack.

When he came through the office door that first day, the first thing I noticed about him was the grin on his face. Later he'd told me it was because he couldn't believe he was going to be playing baseball and making money doing it.

The second thing I noticed was his sport coat. Swear to God, it must have belonged to his father because not only was it about twenty years out of style, it was at least two—maybe three—sizes too small for Jack. The sleeves came about six inches up on his arms, and I looked twice to assure myself there wasn't any hay sticking out of them. To make matters

195

worse, it was a hideous yellow and brown plaid that didn't go at all with his flowered tie, one of those thin ones, the kind *my* dad probably used to wear before I was born.

But, boy! Was he good-looking!

If there hadn't been four years difference in our ages, I would have fallen for him then and there. As it was, I was dating a fellow I'd known in high school and, besides, as soon became evident, girls were the furthest thing from Jack's mind. Baseball was his one and only passion.

Mr. Winthrop, my boss, introduced Jack around to all the people in the office. Of course, everyone already knew who he was. When it came my turn, we said "Hi," shook hands, I smiled, and he blushed. I mean, he turned as red as the red on the Redbirds' uniforms. Now, I'm not bad looking, but you would have thought from the rosy hue on Jack's face he'd been introduced to a famous movie star. Then he was whisked into the general manager's office and was still there when I left for the day.

The next day Mr. Winthrop wanted to watch the rookies work out, along with some other players just up from the lower minors. He asked me to come along to take notes while he dictated. Fortunately, not all my college classes dealt with sociology: I'd also taken shorthand—just in case.

So it happened the first time Jack Murphy stepped onto the field at Cardinal Stadium I was there.

I was sitting in the stands, watching some of the players warming up, tossing balls back and forth when I saw him step out from the dugout. For a good two or three minutes he stood there, his catcher's glove in one hand and his fielder's glove in the other, looking slowly around, drinking in the whole scene: the stadium, the players, the playing field, the groundskeepers, the few people gathered in the stands. When he saw me he grinned, tucked both gloves under one arm, took off his cap, and waved it. I waved back. The manager came over to him and they talked for a while before Jack went to join the other players.

Mr. Winthrop had joined me, bringing with him a six-pack of beer. He offered me one, which I declined.

For the next hour, I kept busy writing down notes on various players while Mr. Winthrop dictated them to me. When Jack's turn came to take batting practice, Mr. Winthrop stopped talking, so I lay my notebook and pencil in my lap and watched.

Jack missed the first pitch by about two feet.

The second pitch he hit . . . oh, about fifteen feet down the third-base line.

Then he stepped out of the batter's box and held the bat up in front of his face. He was talking to himself—or to the bat, I'm not sure which.

After a few moments, he stepped back in.

The next pitch came in and, like a shot, rocketed right back out, clearing the center field fence by a good thirty feet. Mr. Winthrop let out a low whistle.

For the next ten minutes Jack continued a steady barrage of balls flying over the outfield fences—right, center, left—he wasn't particular. By the time he finished, all the other players had stopped what they were doing to watch. The oohs and aahs from the spectators and the other players blew our way when Jack belted out a particularly long home run.

Finally, the manager called the next batter to the plate, and Jack reluctantly turned to carry his bat back to the dugout. Before he got there Mr. Winthrop called him over to where sat.

"Pretty good hitting, kid."

"Thank you, sir."

"I hear you've got a pretty good arm, too."

Jack blushed. "Never had a runner steal a base on me in

three years of high school," he said.

"Impressive. Jack, you know Kitty, here?"

Jack blushed again. "Saw her in the office my first day; nice to meetcha, Miss Kitty."

"Nice to meet you, Jack," I replied.

"I won't keep you from your practice," said Mr. Winthrop. "Keep up the good work."

"Thank you, sir," said Jack. "Miss Kitty," he said to me, doffing his baseball cap.

*****

Jack had a good year for Louisville that season, batting .379, with 36 home runs and 124 runs batted in. His record of throwing out runners slipped slightly from his high school days. Of the sixty-four who attempted to steal second on him, only three were successful. No one even tried to steal third. Had he not been so young, St. Louis would have called him up before the end of the season; also, St. Louis had a pretty decent catcher in Darrell Porter who, at age thirty-two, still had some good years left.

When the season ended, Jack returned home to Oklahoma, where he planned to help his dad on the farm. The Redbird organization wanted him to play winter ball somewhere, but Jack told them his father needed him too badly, and baseball would have to wait until the following spring.

*****

In December we received some devastating news. While walking into town one day, Jack saw a car go off a bridge and into the river. Without hesitating, he dove into the water to try to save whoever might be in the car. It was a young woman and her three small children.

Jack and the mother managed to get two of the children to the river's bank. Jack went back in to get the third child. Just as he reached the car, it shifted and pinned him underneath, crushing both of his legs. Somehow, he managed to get out, get the baby from the back seat, and both made it safely to the river bank.

But Jack's legs were crushed so badly, they had to be amputated. His baseball days were over. He never came back to Louisville.

*****

The next time I saw Jack Murphy was about a year ago. By then, I had become Mrs. Harlan Winthrop. That's right—the same Mr. Winthrop who was my boss in Louisville. So what if there was a twenty-year difference in our ages? By means of shrewd investing in the stock market, Harlan accumulated enough money to start his own minor league baseball team: the Camptown Racers. He was the President and General Manager, while I, who knew absolutely nothing about baseball when I first went to work for the Redbirds some twelve years earlier, was now the Chief Financial Officer. We hired an ex-ballplayer, Sam Finnegan, a local guy from Crownsville, as our Director of Baseball Operations, and were looking for someone to fill the position of Director of Stadium Operations. Sam stood six-foot-four, still weighed a trim two-hundred and thirty pounds, with muscles where I didn't know men had muscles, blond hair, blue eyes; I mean, he was hot! And married. Like me. So that was that.

Then Jack Murphy's application crossed my desk.

It seemed after his baseball career was prematurely terminated, Jack, with the Cardinals paying his way, enrolled at

Oklahoma Baptist University, where he received his Bachelor's degree in Business Administration, and then on to Oklahoma State University, where he got his Masters. For the past five years, he'd served as a Church Business Administrator for a congregation in Lexington. But with a wife and three children to support, the position wasn't paying enough for him to make it on. Besides, baseball was still in his blood.

When he heard about the new team in Camptown, and that we were looking for a Director of Stadium Operations, he immediately sent us his résumé, not realizing Harlan and I were the owners. Naturally, we hired him right away.

Nine months later, Harlan dropped dead of a heart attack. I knew I'd need help running the club and that, while I could assume the position of President, I'd need someone with more baseball knowledge than I had to fill the General Manager's position. It was clear the choice would be between Sam and Jack.

I arranged a dinner meeting at my home with Sam to discuss the situation. After a couple of glasses of wine, I guess I must have given some indication I was attracted to him because the next thing I knew we ended up in bed together. Please understand that, though I'd been happily married to Harlan for nine years, our sex life for the last five of those left much to be desired. Besides, as I said earlier, Sam was a real hunk. The fact he was married with two small children made me feel somewhat guilty, but when I asked him about it he answered that what his wife didn't know wouldn't hurt her.

The next night I had dinner with Jack.

Now, as I mentioned at the beginning of this story, Jack was a real looker, too. And the years had done nothing to take away either those looks or the muscular build I'd seen the first day he walked into the office back in Louisville. In fact, to compensate for the loss of his legs, his upper body had grown even more muscular.

So, I thought . . . why not see if I can get Jack in bed, too, like I did Sam. Okay, there *was* the added perverse aspect that I'd never had sex before with a man with no legs, but I swear that was only incidental.

As I was downing my third glass of wine, and Jack his second cup of coffee—he didn't drink—I told him what my first impressions had been that day back in 1984 when he walked into the office.

Then I said, "So, Jack, how'd you like to go to bed with me?"

He stopped his coffee cup halfway to his lips, peered over the rim at me, then slowly lowered the cup.

"I'm married," he said. "And even if I weren't, you and I *aren't* married. Having sex with you would be sinful either way. I'm sorry but, if that's a prerequisite to getting this job, the best thing for me to do is to submit my resignation."

I wasn't so much embarrassed he turned me down as I was I even asked. I assured him sex wasn't part of the deal, and I was sorry, and it must have been the wine that made me act so forward.

That seemed to placate him, and although the rest of the evening—short as it was—was somewhat strained, we parted on reasonably good terms.

Over the next two weeks, I had Sam over to my house four more times for "conferences," all of which ended up in the bedroom.

Which brings me to today, when I called Sam into my office—not my bedroom—to tell him Jack was getting the job, and he was being fired.

He reacted as I knew he would.

"What! I don't believe this. We've been fucking for the last two weeks, and now you're giving the job to *Jack*? And you're firing *me*? I don't get it!"

"It's pretty simple," I said. "I don't trust you. If you'd cheat on your wife, how do I know you wouldn't cheat on me as the General Manager? I need someone I can trust. You're not it."

Following a string of diatribes, Sam stormed out of my office and out of my life.

In a few moments, Jack will come in, and I'll give him the good news.

He really is a nice guy.

## HOMECOMING
## 1997

Nick stood and walked over to the double glass doors that led out onto his balcony. The apartment took up the entire third floor of the building that had replaced his great-great grandfather's livery in 1913. He looked across the street to the sidewalk in front of the Tipsy Toad Bar and Grill, to the exact spot where his great-grandfather, Will, had shined Abraham Lincoln's boots a century and a half earlier.

He had just finished looking at coins and documents, some of which had been in his family for one-hundred-and-fifty-years: an IOU received by nine-year-old Will in 1847 from Abraham Lincoln in lieu of payment for the shoeshine; a letter sent in 1863 by Will to his wife, Rebecca, the day before he was killed in the battle of Chickamauga, describing his encounter with Lincoln that produced the IOU; a second letter sent to Will by Lincoln the day he was assassinated; and the two coins that accompanied Lincoln's letter, one an 1847 one-cent piece, sent as payment for the IOU, the other a fifty-cent piece dated 1865, with an "S" mintmark, a coin so rare that, according to coin catalogs, it never existed.

*One-hundred-and-fifty-years* thought Nick. *So many changes. So many memories. So many stories.*

He slid the door opened and stepped outside. A gentle

breeze wound its way down Main Street, giving the air a clean, refreshing feeling. Temperatures in Kentucky in July could sometimes be unbearable, but this weekend's weather, other than a slight chance of rain for tomorrow, was forecast to be perfect for *Homecoming*.

Each July 4th for the past six years Camptown had celebrated *Homecoming*. It started in 1991, when Nick's son, Matt, and Brad Rickman both returned home the same day— July 3rd—from serving in Desert Storm.

The event proved so popular it became a regular happening.

This year's *Homecoming* was especially significant. The town was celebrating the one-hundred-and-fiftieth anniversary of its founding. Nick's great-great-grandfather, Jeremiah Van Pelt, was one of those founding fathers. His livery stable was the second structure in town, built two months after the Tipsy Toad.

This was the old section of town now, the historic section, the one where the tourists came to browse through the antique and craft shops; to have lunch at the Tipsy Toad, where John L. Sullivan once slaked his thirst; to wander through the museum at the Historical Society. Other than the newspaper office, built last year after the old one burned down, there wasn't a building on the block—more like the equivalent of two normal city blocks—that was less than seventy-five years old. In fact, up until a few years ago, Nick's building which, in addition to his apartment now housed the law offices of Townsend, Rafferty, and Parmele, was still referred to as that "new" building!

He looked toward the end of the block where a huge banner with the word HOMECOMING was strung high above the street from the new offices of the *Chickapea Southern Gazette* to the building that held the Historical Society and the museum, which Nick's wife, Dolly, was, at that moment, preparing to close up. At the other end of the street hung a second banner that read 150 YEARS CELEBRATION, stretching from the Claiborne Hotel to the Chickapea County Bank.

A few blocks over on Market Street Nick could see the steeple of St. Timothy's Catholic Church peeking through the maple trees. Beyond that, out toward the edge of town, another steeple was evident, this one belonging to the Chickapea Baptist Church.

The street was filled with people on this evening before the Fourth, tourists, and former residents who had returned for the weekend's festivities. Nick watched one family, visitors he surmised since he didn't recognize them, as they peered through the window of Amy Morton's "Teddy Bear Antiques" shop. A small boy of about five or six standing behind them was more interested in the five-foot-high bronze statue of Tom, a wild turkey who became the hero of Camptown in 1911 when he saved a little girl from being dragged off by a cougar.

His reverie was interrupted by the sound of a voice from the sidewalk below.

"Nick!"

Nick bent over the balcony railing to see Mayor Townsend standing there.

"Richard! How are you this glorious evening?"

"I'm fine, thanks. Sorry to hear about your dad. Mr. Jacobson tells me there's not going to be a service, that he's going to be cremated."

"A memorial service . . . we're having a memorial service next weekend."

"Let me know—I'd like to come."

"You bet."

Nick watched as Richard continued on down the street, and became hidden in the shadows of the buildings on either side. It would be dark soon. He glanced at his watch: five minutes till nine. Dolly would be home shortly and they'd be leaving to drive up to Louisville to pick up their son and daughter-in-law at the airport. Matt and Erin were bringing the newest addition to the family, three-month-old Jerome. Dolly was excited—as was he, he had to admit—at the news the kids were coming back for Homecoming. This would be the first time they'd meet their new grandson.

Nick started to go back inside when a movement on the street below caught his eye. He looked and, in the gathering dusk, saw a tall, lanky man on horseback coming down the middle of Main Street, a Main Street, Nick realized, no longer paved, but, rather, one of dirt, and seemingly deserted. When the man arrived at the Tipsy Toad he stopped his horse, dismounted, and began talking with a young boy, a boy who looked strangely familiar—as did the man. Then Nick realized who they were: his great-grandfather Will and Abraham Lincoln!

As suddenly as the two men had appeared, they vanished and a group of men wearing clothes the likes of which Nick had seen only in old Sears and Roebuck catalogs came pouring out of the Tipsy Toad. One man appeared to be the center of attention. Nick knew from pictures he'd seen at the Historical Society, of which he was the president, it was John L. Sullivan. The men came to an abrupt halt as a wild turkey—at least four feet high—sauntered past them.

Nick blinked his eyes—and the street was filled with people again. But not the same crowd as there moments before. These were women in Garibaldi dresses escorted by men in bowler hats and top hats. A young girl used a stick to roll a wooden hoop about two and a half feet in diameter.   Two boys wrestled in the middle of the street.

"Nick?"

Nick turned at the sound of Dolly's voice. "I'm out . . ." he started to answer, then smiled. In spite of being married for almost thirty years, there were still times when he forgot his wife was deaf. He'd have to go back inside to greet her.

When he looked back to the street, everything was gone. Like his great-grandfather and Mr. Lincoln, the crowd of men from the Tipsy Toad and the turkey, the men and women from—from what era?—had vanished. Main Street as he knew it was back: paved and filled with present-day tourists.

Nick shook his head. Perhaps it was true, what they said: the ghosts of Camptown never really leave, but live on in the hearts and minds and memories of those who come after.

He took one more look at the town he loved so much, that was a part of him and of his family, turned and went inside and slid the door shut behind him.

His thoughts of a few minutes earlier came rushing back to him: *so many changes; so many memories; so many stories.*

And so many more to be told.

# APPENDIX A

Following is a partial list of characters that appear in the stories in this book. Names listed in *italics* indicate that the name was not actually used in the story. The word **NARRATOR** following a character's name indicates that, in first-person stories, that person is the narrator; in third-person stories the story is told from that person's point of view or that character is the main character.

Years of birth and death, where known, are shown in the alphabetical listing, Appendix B.

\*\*\*\*\*\*\*\*\*\*\*\*\*\*\*\*\*\*\*\*\*\*\*\*\*\*\*\*\*\*\*\*\*\*\*\*\*\*\*\*\*\*\*\*\*\*\*\*\*\*\*\*\*\*

*The IOU*

> LINCOLN, Abraham
> VAN PELT, Jeremiah
> VAN PELT, Nicholas "Nick" - **NARRATOR**
> VAN PELT, William "Will"

*Camptown Races*

> FOSTER, *Stephen*
> *FREEMAN*, George - **NARRATOR**
> LUCY
> MAGUIRE, *Zadok*
> MARBURY, *Stanford*
> ROBERTS, Jig
> *WILLIAMSON*, Dolores
> *WILLIAMSON*, Ethel
> *WILLIAMSON*, Howard

*After The Battle*

CARTEE, Ruland "Roo" - **NARRATOR**
COLE, Olivia
COLE, Owen

*The Lynching Of Moses Morgan*

MCCORMICK, *Obadiah* - **NARRATOR**
MCCORMICK, Emily
SWANEY, William J. "Billy"
WINETROPP, *Gordon*
WINETROPP, *Lucinda*

*The Day I Whipped John L. Sullivan*

CLAIBORNE, *Mordecai*
MCCORKLE, *Henry* "Hank" - **NARRATOR**
MULLANEY, *Artis*
SULLIVAN, John L.
TOWNSEND, *Wilbur*

*The Poker Game*

*BIDDLEMIRE*, Andy - **NARRATOR**
COLE, *Owen*
JACOBSON, *Hugh*
*JAMIESON*, Elly
ONE-EYED MAN
PREACHERMAN
TOWNSEND, *Wilbur*

209

*Tom*

BIDDLEMIRE, *Homer*
BUHLIG, Gunther
BUHLIG, *Hannah*
BUHLIG, Katrina
CLAIBORNE, Eunice
JINX
LEWIS, Wilford
LIMPKE, Ezra
*MCBAIN, Scooter* - **NARRATOR**
MCCORKLE, *Garnet*
MULLANEY, *Perk*
O'BRIEN, *Patrick* "Paddy" *Gilligan*
OGLEMAN, *Levi*
POMEROY, *Milton*
TOM

*Woolly Wanda*

*LISTERMAN*, Wanda
*MCCORKLE, Henry*
*MCCORKLE*, Marcus - **NARRATOR**
STEARMAN, Candy

*My Grandfather's Grandfather Clock*

*BIDDLEMIRE*, Danny
*TOWNSEND*, Annabel
*TOWNSEND*, Buck - **NARRATOR**
*TOWNSEND*, Edgar
*TOWNSEND, Lyric* - narrator's grandmother
TOWNSEND, Wilbur Eugene

*When The Leaves Fall*

  *CARTEE*, Angela
  CARTEE, *Emma* - narrator's grandmother
  CARTEE, *George* - narrator's grandfather
  *CARTEE, Glen* - narrator's father
  *CARTEE, Marietta* - narrator's mother
  *CARTEE*, Michael
  *CARTEE*, Patrick
  *CARTEE*, Rosemarie (Nana) - **NARRATOR**
  *CLAIBORNE*, Eunice

*The Male Pooch Barn*

  EVERINGHAM, Chadwick
  MCGINNIS, Howard
  MCGINNIS, Humphrey
  STANTON, Cornelius
  *STANTON, Cornelius, Jr.* "Junior" - **NARRATOR**
  *STANTON*, Jewel
  *STANTON*, Rachel
  *STANTON*, Tom

*Down In The River*

  GOODMAN, Merle - **NARRATOR**
  JOHNSON, Lorelei

*I Never Saw The Color Blue*

> *KITCHEN*, Bonnie - **NARRATOR**
> *KITCHEN,* Dolly
> *KITCHEN*, Molly
> THORESON, Billy

*Numbers*

> GILLESPIE, Allan - **NARRATOR**
> *GILLESPIE*, Joanne
> O'KEARNEY, *Eugene*
> THORNTON, Richard J. T.

*Full Court*

> *MORTON*, Roger, Jr.
> *STACEY*, Mildred
> *TOLBERT,* Leslie "Les" - **NARRATOR**

*Hope*

> *NORMAN*, Hope
> *RAFFERTY, April May* "Sister Martin"
> *ST. JOHN*, Marcy - **NARRATOR**

*Sister Martin*

> O'KEARNEY, Eugene
> RAFFERTY, April May "Sister Martin"
> STERNMAN, Oscar
> TOLBERT, Jim
> YOUNG, *Merle* - **NARRATOR**

212

*Rolling Pins, Quince Pies, and the Devil's Playground*

    BAILEY, *Alice*
    COLE, Rebecca
    COLE, Katherine – **NARRATOR**
    MCNAMARA, Eulacinda "Diggy"
    SISTER ABIGAIL
    YOUNG, Merle

*Morchellas*

    *YOUNG, Eldred* - **NARRATOR**

*Angels In The Christmas Tree*

    *PARMELE*, Linda
    *PARMELE, Paul* – **NARRATOR**
    *PARMELE-RICKMAN*, Angel
    *PARMELE-RICKMAN,* Jennie
    *RICKMAN*, Brad
    *SMART, Arthur* - doctor

*The Pool Boy*

    *LINDHURST*, Eddie
    MARTIN, *Olga* - **NARRATOR**

*The Empty Closet*

    JEFFERS, David - **NARRATOR**
    TOWNSEND, Richard

*Nice Guys . . .*

    FINNEGAN, Sam
    MURPHY, Jack
    WINTHROP, Harlan
    *WINTHROP, Katherine* "Kitty" - **NARRATOR**

*Homecoming*

    LINCOLN, Abraham
    SULLIVAN, John L.
    TOWNSEND, Richard
    *VAN PELT*, Dolly
    *VAN PELT, Nicholas* "Nick" – **NARRATOR**
    VAN PELT, *William* "Will"

# APPENDIX B

Following is a partial list of character that appear in the stories indicated following their name. First or last names in italics denote the name was not actually used in the story indicated. Following each name are that character's years of birth and death, where known. If the year of death is left blank, that person was still known to be alive in 2022.

\*\*\*\*\*\*\*\*\*\*\*\*\*\*\*\*\*\*\*\*\*\*\*\*\*\*\*\*\*\*\*\*\*\*\*\*\*\*\*\*\*\*\*\*\*\*\*\*\*\*\*\*\*\*\*\*\*\*
\*\*\*\*\*\*\*

BAILEY, *Alice* (1905-1977) *Rolling Pins, Quince Pies, and the Devil's Playground*
BIDDLEMIRE, Andy (1869-1895) *The Poker Game,*
BIDDLEMIRE, Danny (1896-1939) *My Grandfather's Grandfather Clock*
BIDDLEMIRE, *Homer* (1835-1937) *Tom*
BUHLIG, Gunther 1904-1916) *Tom*
BUHLIG, *Hannah* (1883-1938) *Tom*
BUHLIG, Katrina (1909- ?) *Tom*
CARTEE, Angela (1923-1941) *When The Leaves Fall*
CARTEE, *Emma* (1875-1945) *When The Leaves Fall* – narrator's grandmother
CARTEE, *George* (1865-1937) *When The Leaves Fall* – narrator's grandfather
CARTEE, *Glen* (1899-1965) *When The Leaves Fall* – narrator's father
CARTEE, *Marietta* (1900-1972) *When The Leaves Fall* - narrator's mother
CARTEE, Michael (1927-1947) *When The Leaves Fall*
CARTEE, Patrick (1927- ) *When The Leaves Fall*
CARTEE, Rosemarie (Nana) (1921-1993) *When The Leaves Fall*

215

CARTEE, Ruland "Roo" (1821-1876) *After The Battle*
CLAIBORNE, Eunice (1851-1936) *Tom, When The Leaves Fall*
CLAIBORNE, *Mordecai* (1822-1883) *The Day I Whipped John L. Sullivan* - hotel owner
COLE, Katherine (1962-   ) *Rolling Pins, Quince Pies, and the Devil's Playground*
COLE, Olivia (1834-1885) *After The Battle*
 COLE, Owen (1854-1902) *After The Battle, The Poker Game*
COLE, Rebecca (1912-1994) *Rolling Pins, Quince Pies, and the Devil's Playground*
EVERINGHAM, Chadwick ( ? - ? ) *The Male PoochBarn*
FINNEGAN, Sam (1960-   ) *Nice Guys.*
FOSTER, *Stephen* (1826-1864) *Camptown Races*
FREEMAN, George (ca. 1836-1938) *Camptown Races*
GILLESPIE, Allan (1905-1968) *Numbers*
GILLESPIE, Joanne (1909-1980) *Numbers*
GOODMAN, Merle (1896-1943) *Down In The River*
JACOBSON, Hugh (1827-1899) *The Poker Game*
JAMIESON, Elly (1852-1909) *The Poker Game*
JEFFERS, David (1956-1992) *The Empty Closet*
JOHNSON, Lorelei (1928-1943) *Down In The River*
KITCHEN, Bonnie (1942-   ) *I Never Saw The Color Blue*
KITCHEN, Dolly (1944-   ) *I Never Saw The Color Blue*
KITCHEN, Dolly (see *VAN PELT*, Dolly)-*Homecoming*
KITCHEN, Molly (1944-    ) *I Never Saw The Color Blue*
LEWIS, Wilford (1874-1917) *Tom*
LIMPKE, Ezra ( ? -  ? ) *Tom*
LINCOLN, Abraham (1809-1865) *The IOU, Homecoming*
LINDHURST, Eddie (1966-1995) *The Pool Boy*
LISTERMAN, Wanda (1907-1990) *Woolly Wanda*
MAGUIRE, Zadok ( ? - ? ) *Camptown Races*
MARBURY, *Stanford* ( ? - ? ) *Camptown Races*
MARTIN, *Olga* (1942-1995) *The Pool Boy*

MCBAIN, Scooter (1860-1920) *The Day I Whipped John L. Sullivan, Tom*

MCCORKLE, *Garnet* (1883-1966) *Tom*

MCCORKLE, Henry "Hank" (1860-1923) *The Day I Whipped John L. Sullivan, Woolly Wanda* – narrator's father

MCCORKLE, Marcus (1907-1944) *Woolly Wanda*

MCCORMICK, *Creek* (1897-1974) *The Lynching of Moses Morgan*

MCCORMICK, Emily (1904-1970) *The Lynching of Moses Morgan*

MCGINNIS, *Howard* (1880-1948) *The Male Pooch Barn*

MCGINNIS, Humphrey (1907-1945) *The Male Pooch Barn*

MCNAMARA, Eulacinda "Diggy"(1888-1973) *Rolling Pins, Quince Pies, and the Devil's Playground*

MORGAN, Leafy (? -1869) *The Lynching of Moses Morgan*

MORGAN, Moses (1832-1869) *The Lynching of Moses Morgan*

MORTON, Roger, Jr. (1954-1990) *Full Court*

MULLANEY, *Perk* (1838-1913) *Tom*

MURPHY, Jack (1966-   ) *Nice Guys . . .*

NORMAN, Hope (1956- ?) *Hope*

O'BRIEN, *Patrick* "Paddy" *Gilligan* (1885-1958) *Tom*

OGLEMAN, *Levi* (1850-1907) *The Poker Game, Tom*

O'KEARNEY, *Eugene* (1916-1997) *Numbers, Sister Martin*

PARMELE, Linda (1953-   ) *Angels In The Christmas Tree*

PARMELE, *Paul* (1951-   ) *Angels In The Christmas Tree, Homecoming*

PARMELE-RICKMAN, Angel (1996-   ) *Angels In The Christmas Tree*

PARMELE-RICKMAN, Jennie (1976-   ) *Angels In The Christmas Tree*

POMEROY, *Milton* (1876-1918) *Tom*

RAFFERTY, *April May* "Sister Martin" (1948-1993) *Hope, Sister Martin*

RICKMAN, Brad (1973-   ) *Angels In The Christmas Tree*

ROBERTS, Jig (? - ?) *Camptown Races*

217

SISTER ABIGAIL (actual name unknown) (1873-1979) *Rolling Pins, Quince Pies, and the Devil's Playground*

SMART, Artis (? - ?) *Angels in the Christmas Tree (doctor)*

STACEY, Mildred (1922-1988) *Full Court*

STANTON, Cornelius (1888-1947) *The Male Pooch Barn*

STANTON, Cornelius, Jr. "Junior" (1909-1965) *The Male Pooch Barn*

STANTON, Jewel (1887-1947) *The Male Pooch Barn*

STANTON, Rachel (1912-1932) *The Male Pooch Barn*

STANTON, Tom (1913-1987) *The Male Pooch Barn*

STEARMAN, Candy (1857-1931) *Woolly Wanda*

STERNMAN, Oscar (1929-   ) *Sister Martin*

ST. JOHN, Marcy (? - ?) *Hope*

SULLIVAN, John L. (1858-1918) *The Day I Whipped John L. Sullivan, Homecoming*

SWANEY, William J. "Billy" (1850-?) *The Lynching of Moses Morgan*

THORESON, Billy (1942-?) *I Never Saw The Color Blue*

THORNTON, Richard J. T. (1919-1977) *Numbers*

TOLBERT, Jim (1928-1996) *Sister Martin*

TOLBERT, Leslie "Les" (1953-   ) *Full Court*

TOWNSEND, Annabel (1814-1839) *My Grandfather's Grandfather Clock*

TOWNSEND, Buck (1896-1945) *My Grandfather's Grandfather Clock*

TOWNSEND, Edgar (1866-1939) *My Grandfather's Grandfather Clock*

TOWNSEND, Lyric (1834-1935) *My Grandfather's Grandfather Clock* - narrator's grandmother

TOWNSEND, Richard (1954-   ) *The Empty Closet, Homecoming*

TOWNSEND, Wilbur Eugene (1832-1922) *The Day I Whipped John L. Sullivan, The Poker Game, My Grandfather's Grandfather Clock*

*VAN PELT,* Dolly - *(see KITCHEN,* Dolly*)* (1944-   )
*Homecoming*
*VAN PELT, Jeremiah* (1816-1860) *The IOU*  - Will's father
*VAN PELT,* Micah (1861-1898) *The IOU*
*VAN PELT, Nicholas* "Nick" (1943-   ) *The IOU, Homecoming*
*VAN PELT,* William "Will" (1838-1863) *The IOU, Homecoming*
WINETROPP, *Gordon* (1872-1940) *The Lynching of Moses*
*Morgan*
WINETROPP, *Lucinda* (1874-1941) *The Lynching of Moses*
*Morgan*
WINTHROP, Harlan (1942-1996) *Nice Guys . . .*
*WINTHROP, Katherine* "Kitty" (1962-   ) *Nice Guys . . .*
YOUNG, Merle (1946-   ) *Sister Martin, Rolling Pins, Quince Pies,*
*and the Devil's Playground,*
YOUNG, Eldred (1939-1982*) Morchellas*


NAMES OF UNKNOWN & NON-HUMAN
CHARACTERS


LUCY (? - 1862) *Camptown Races*
ONE-EYED MAN (? - ?) *The Poker Game*
PREACHERMAN  (? - ?) *The Poker Game*
TOM (? - 1911) *Tom*

219

## ABOUT THE AUTHOR

 A retired Lutheran minister, Kenn has served congregations in Indiana, Kentucky, and Missouri. In 2000 he sold his wedding business in Maui, Hawaii, and retired to Lower Northern Michigan (Ernest Hemingway country), where he and his wife, Judy, also a retired minister, both in their eighties, along with their fourteen-year-old dog, Louie (fifty percent Beagle, twenty-five percent Samoyed, twenty-five percent Old English Sheepdog) grow gracefully old together, living the good life in their cabin on Deer Lake.

www.ingramcontent.com/pod-product-compliance
Lightning Source LLC
Chambersburg PA
CBHW021243260626
47155CB00004BA/1285